Key West Dreams

Key West Dreams

A Novel

N. E. Julian

Contents

Prologue

No Weak Sisters in This House

On a cold, raw afternoon in early November, eight year old Sarah Ann Fitzpatrick trudged home from another difficult day at St. Michael the Avenging Angel Grade School. Although Sarah Ann could read at the level of a high school student, St. Michael's had no accelerated program for gifted children; the child spent her time at school in a fog of boredom in a crowded classroom overflowing with third-graders. Earlier that afternoon during literature class, as the other children stumbled through the paragraphs that they were expected to read out loud, Sarah Ann had succumbed to temptation and begun stealthily reading a library book that she had hidden in her lap. Her usual pastime of paging ahead in the text was foreclosed since she had already read the entire book.

When Sister Dolores Marie called upon Sarah Ann, the girl was engrossed in the adventures of Freddy the pig, a talking porcine detective who solved gentle puzzles in a series of young adult novels, and had lost her place in the textbook. The nun, a withered bride of Christ who in the earthly realm had sole responsibility every school day for 48 active children from 8:00 a.m. to 3:00 p.m. without even a teacher's aide for help, embarrassed Sarah Ann in front of the whole class by telling her that little girls who didn't pay attention added more lashes to the scourging that Jesus had suffered on behalf of sinners like herself—especially since Sarah Ann had been admonished earlier in the week for reading her older sister's copy of 'Lord of the Flies' during history class. The other children had stared at Sarah Ann with the horrified, you're going to hell looks that she had been receiving from her fellow students since the first grade.

I want Mom, Sarah Ann thought as she entered the front door of her parents' small rowhouse in an aging Philadelphia neighborhood whose gentrification was years in the future. But her mother wasn't there. Francis X. Fitzpatrick, Sarah Ann's father, had finally been forced by his wife's doctors to admit her to the Eastern Pennsylvania Psychiatric Institute that morning.

Sara Ann knew that her mother had been acting strangely for weeks. Evelyn Fitzpatrick would wander from room to room in the family's house, crying and confused, her mind so muddled from severe depression that she couldn't decide what to wear or what to do. When Sarah Ann came home from school each day, her mother was usually sitting in her nightgown at the kitchen table, chain-smoking and staring vacantly at the dirty breakfast dishes that still littered the table.

Sarah Ann's father resisted getting any treatment for his wife other than a weekly appointment with her psychiatrist. "She'll get over it," Mr. Fitzpatrick would say coldly to his daughters as his wife sobbed heartbrokenly in the bedroom. "We all know this has happened before. Just ignore her." His only concession to his wife's illness was making his oldest daughter, thirteen year old Mariclaire, stay home from school to babysit her mother on Mrs. Fitzpatrick's really bad days.

The family had settled into an uneasy routine. Each morning as he left for work, Mr. Fitzpatrick put his razor blades into his suit pocket to prevent his wife from slitting her wrists while her husband and daughters were gone for the day.

In the afternoons of the days she was allowed to go to school, Mariclaire straightened the house and then fixed dinner. The next daughter, eleven year old Laura Ann, did the laundry and ironed her father's dress shirts. Both girls had survived their mother's previous breakdowns and knew what their father expected them to do, although Mariclaire seethed with anger at having to be her siblings' surrogate mother and Laurie was ashamed of her mother's bizarre behavior.

Sarah Ann was responsible for ensuring that she and the youngest Fitzpatrick girl, Olivia Ann who was six, had fresh underwear and the clean white blouses needed to accompany their Catholic school uniforms. Since neither Sarah nor Olivia had acquired the personal fastidiousness that would distinguish them in later years, they often skipped their evening baths and wore the same underwear for days at a time. As the weeks passed and their mother's depression deepened, the two little girls became increasingly scruffy, but no one noticed.

Mrs. Fitzpatrick's recurring breakdowns hadn't made much of an impression on Sarah Ann in the past, despite the fact that one of her earliest memories was of her mother sitting on the stairs and sobbing desperately as she clutched Sarah to her chest. Now, though, Sarah was acutely aware that everything was wrong; the mother whom she loved more than anyone had collapsed and, because of her family's conspiracy of silence, no one would tell her what was happening. So Sarah Ann tried to help—she continually told her mother that she loved her and gave her cheap presents from the dime store in a pathetic attempt to make her mother stop crying.

The family's uneasy equilibrium broke that gray fall day when Evelyn Fitzpatrick, who was alone in the house, swallowed a bottle of aspirin in a half-hearted suicide attempt, then called her husband at work to tell him what she had done. Francis Fitzpatrick's glacial wall of denial was finally pierced; from his law office he called the police who rushed his wife to the hospital to have her stomach pumped.

When Mr. Fitzpatrick arrived at the emergency room, he acceded to the doctors' and cops' demands that he sign the papers for his wife's involuntary commitment to EPPI. Since the U.S. Supreme Court hadn't yet issued its series of misguided rulings granting the mentally ill the right to determine their own treatment, Evelyn Fitzpatrick, who always became more obstinate as she became more ill, wasn't required to consent.

So Sarah Ann now stood in her family's living room, which, like her father, was shabby, cold and dispirited. "Where's Mommy?" she demanded.

"Your mother is in the hospital."

"What's wrong? Is she sick?"

Mr. Fitzpatrick, who never discussed his wife's problems with his younger children or even acknowledged to them that anything was wrong no matter how bizarrely his wife was acting, said evasively, "Your mother needs to be away for a while."

"A while? How long is that?" Sarah Ann asked fearfully.

"Your mother may not be home for several months," Mr. Fitzpatrick said frigidly.

Sarah started to cry. "I won't see Mommy for two months?" she asked sadly.

"What have I told you about crying, Sarah Ann?" Mr. Fitzpatrick said demandingly. "Crying is for sissies and I'm not having any weak sisters in this house.

"If you're upset you should act like Mariclaire. She isn't weak—she gets mad, not sad. Now go in the kitchen and help your sisters get dinner."

Sarah Ann stared at her father, tears running silently down her small face from under her glasses. She knew she wasn't allowed to cry but she couldn't stop the hateful tears from leaking out of her eyes.

Francis Fitzpatrick made no attempt to comfort or reassure his child. "Well," he said coldly, "I guess you really love your mother." He turned and started to walk away. Sarah Ann felt that loving her mother was another indication that she was shamefully weak.

"Daddy," she said.

Mr. Fitzpatrick stopped walking and turned to face his daughter. "What?"

"My feet hurt. Mommy never got me new shoes this fall and last year's shoes are too small." She looked down at her scuffed oxfords, feeling their pressure against the ends of her toes.

"God bless you, Sarah Ann," Mr. Fitzpatrick, who seldom overtly swore, said harshly. "Your mother's in a mental hospital and you're whining to me about new shoes. I don't know how I'm going to pay the bills for your mother's treatment and keep on feeding you children so don't bother me about new shoes. Now do what I told you—go to the kitchen and help your sisters."

Mr. Fitzpatrick turned angrily from his daughter. "I'm sorry, Daddy," she whispered to his retreating back as he walked away from her.

Sarah Ann walked slowly to the kitchen. Not even his wife's incarceration in a mental hospital would cause Francis Fitzpatrick to bend his rule that his family did not eat in restaurants, so Laurie was peeling potatoes while Mariclaire mixed up a meatloaf.

"They're going to give Mom shock treatments," Mariclaire said to Laurie in a matter-of-fact, almost emotionless tone of voice.

"Shock treatments? What are those?" Laurie asked.

"Dad said the doctors will stick electric wires in her and make her have convulsions. It's supposed to make the depression get better."

"Serves her right for being crazy," Laurie said angrily. "What if my friends find out my mother's in a nut house."

"No," Sarah Ann said from the kitchen door. "No."

"No, what?" Mariclaire asked as she eyed her younger sister with distaste.

"They're not going to give Mommy electric shocks."

"Oh yeah—what do you know about anything?" Mariclaire demanded. "Did Dad tell you something different?"

"No," Sarah had to admit, stunned at the idea that doctors were going to place electric wires on her mother and zap her into seizures.

"Well Dad told me they'll be giving her shock treatments every day for a week or two since they can't wait for the pills to start working." Mariclaire turned and looked more closely at her sister. "God, you're a mess. Why is your face so dirty?"

Sarah Ann looked helplessly at her two older sisters, realizing that they would give her no comfort. "We had art today at school," she answered. "I got chalk on my hands. I guess some of it got on my face."

"Well go get cleaned up," Mariclaire snapped. "And take off your uniform and put on some slacks. And where's Olivia?"

"She's playing Barbies with the kids next door," Laurie answered.

"Good. I hope she stays there for a while."

Sarah Ann trudged slowly from the kitchen to the bathroom where she washed her face and hands and cleaned off her tear-spattered glasses. She walked across the hall into the small bedroom she and Olivia shared.

Sarah turned on the bedroom light, then pushed the shabby green-painted bookshelves across the door so that it couldn't be opened. Still wearing her blue-plaid school uniform, she curled up in a frightened ball on top of the ratty old iron bed with the lumpy sagging mattress she had inherited from Laura Ann when their father upgraded his two older daughters to cheap bed frames and foam-slab mattresses from Sears. Not for the Fitzpatrick girls were the fairy-princess rooms with white canopy beds that were then in vogue.

Sarah Ann held her two small troll dolls, Fat Fred and Short Mort, one in each clenched little fist. They were her two best friends that year. She lay on the bed, rigid with fear and anxiety, desperately wanting her mother, as the cold dreary afternoon dragged to a close. Finally she fell asleep.

Seven weeks later Evelyn Fitzpatrick came home from the hospital. While she was away, their father took Sarah Ann and Olivia to visit their mother one time. Mariclaire and Laurie refused to go. Sarah, who had a vivid imagination and no one in whom to confide her fears, was afraid to enter the gloomy brick EPPI facilities. She thought that awful things would be happening to her mother and might possibly happen to her.

However, when she walked timidly into the patients' day room, clutching a cheap African violet she had bought out of her allowance for her mother, she saw that the room's beige walls and nondescript furniture had a sad, ordinary drabness that reminded her of her parents' house. Looking around the large room, she saw other frightened children visiting hospitalized parents, sullen teenagers covering their heartache with angry contempt, and bewildered spouses trying to make uncomfortable conversation with their drugged and subdued mates.

When visiting hours were over, Sarah's constant, morbid fears for her mother were alleviated. She knew that her mother would be coming home.

When Evelyn Fitzpatrick was finally released from the hospital, she had been brain-burned into a state of constant, manic cheerfulness. She talked incessantly and chain-smoked constantly while visiting with the neighbors and friends who called on her. Her daughters still ran the house.

Mrs. Fitzpatrick's electrical high gradually subsided; slowly she began to function again as wife and mother. By late spring conditions in the Fitzpatrick household had returned to what passed for normal in the unhappy Fitzpatrick marriage and the parents' uneasy relations with their children.

Like her two older sisters, though, Sarah Ann now realized that the stable times wouldn't last. In a year, or perhaps two or at most three years, her mother would have another breakdown, and then another, and then another. The knowledge haunted Sarah; she began to feel a constant sense of impending doom that no favorable event could alleviate for long. The only time she attempted to discuss her fears with her father, his response was to say angrily, "You're so damn sensitive," and then change the subject. She never brought up the matter again.

As the years passed, Evelyn Fitzpatrick's recurring depressions worsened. She began having psychotic episodes in which she would rave and hallucinate and babble incessantly. Francis Fitzpatrick became even colder and more withdrawn, more shabby and more eccentric. He threw all his energies into his fanatical, tormented Catholicism, his law practice and various causes; while he attempted to single-handedly end the Vietnam War, Sarah Ann became an expert at force-feeding and forcibly washing and dressing her mother. Mr. Fitzpatrick's principal response to his wife's worsening condition was to start knocking her around when she was particularly recalcitrant. He continued to resist hospitalizing her so that Sarah Ann would have to place the phone calls to her mother's psychiatrist and beg that he insist upon her mother's admission to the hospital.

Sarah Ann felt a constant sense of sadness. As she lost her childhood and then her adolescence and young adult years to her family's problems, she coped by transforming herself from the child Sarah, who grieved, into the adult Sally, whose façade of cheerfully ironic good manners masked a woman who seldom felt much of anything aside from flashes of the anger and irritability Mr. Fitzpatrick had so carefully inculcated in his children.

Chapter One

A Parrot Head In Pearls

"You Went and Got Rich"

Sally Ann Fitzpatrick Stanton moodily drank iced tea while writing her "Ode to Betrayal (IV)." The breach of faith in question was her recent discovery that her idol, Jimmy Buffett, self-styled "pirate songster of Key West," was now a driven millionaire businessman.

Sally Ann had nothing against rich people. She hadn't inherited her father's belief that only material deprivation and martyred resignation would keep her out of the Catholic hell he so deeply feared, but in which she didn't believe. Although, like her father, she was a lawyer, unlike him she hadn't sabotaged her career by rejecting every opportunity to earn more than the professional equivalent of a subsistence wage. She earned a good salary as a corporate attorney, and would gladly have taken any pay raises her company offered her. Also unlike her father, who had deeply loved his career but who had thought it was a sin to make money, Sally Ann despised her job but did it to earn a living.

Jimmy Buffett, though, had been Sally Ann's role model in her quest to change her compulsive life. Along with his millions of other

Parrot Head fans (similar to the Dead Head fans of the late Jerry Garcia but with more of a sense of humor), she had worshiped the image of the island cowboy drinking margaritas, using it to stoke her own dreams of a relaxing life far from the dreary tedium of the corporate world.

Sally Ann ran her pearl necklace through her fingers, then let it rest against her cream silk blouse. She wondered if she had let down her naturally-suspicious guard only to be taken in by a façade sheltering another stress-ridden entrepreneur. Was her favorite singer the entertainment world's equivalent of the yuppie bikers who roared around Philadelphia's upper-middle class watering holes on Saturdays on their Harleys, masquerading as well-groomed Hell's Angels with Filofaxes?

She finished "Ode (IV)" (her previous compositions I through III having nothing to do with the entertainer) and dedicated it: "To Jimmy Buffett—you went and got rich, you son of a bitch." She drank some more iced tea and looked at the large oil painting on the restaurant's front wall, enjoying the sight of the men and women in the painted party scene drinking and smoking with unfashionable abandon. After paying her lunch tab and leaving a good tip, Sally Ann left the Twentieth Street Bar and Grill, waving to the hostess and the gay waiters who comprised the serving staff at her favorite restaurant. She stepped into the mild sunshine of a cheerful spring day.

On her way back to the office, Sally Ann strolled behind a tall Philadelphia policeman, admiring the set of his shoulders and his tight butt in his dark blue cop trousers. Citizen's arrest, officer, she thought. I'll need to pat you down.

Sally Ann smiled as the policeman turned down a side street. She continued to walk demurely back to her office, hiding her eyes behind sunglasses as she watched her fellow pedestrians. Aside from the cop, there was a dearth of good-looking men, since she didn't find either spindly corporate drones or the pot-bellied descendants of the short Mediterranean people who had immigrated to the East Coast in the early 1900s to be attractive.

Her tastes ran to men who looked like her husband: tall, masculine, with cleft chins and signs of a heavy beard, muscular hairy forearms, hard-palmed hands, broad shoulders and great rear ends. She was attracted to males who, also like her husband, showed a discreet patch of heavy chest hair above the open collars of their sports shirts, although she disliked the south Philly and Jersey cretins who wore unbuttoned shirts open to their abdomens with multiple heavy gold chains dangling on their furred torsos.

Sally Ann was happily married and didn't fool around. But, as she often thought, if God didn't want her to notice good-looking men, why had He given her eyes (nearsighted though they were). Thanks to her contacts, she had 20/20 vision, which she focused as frequently as possible on male faces and bodies while shielding her thoughts behind her pale, refined face.

She kept on walking. Despite taking the most circuitous route through Center City, Sally Ann arrived too soon at the sixth circle of hell, otherwise known as the corporation where she worked. Her place of employment would have been hell's seventh circle except that her salary helped pay the first and second mortgages on her house, and Sally Ann liked her home extremely well.

She sighed and entered the building's lobby. Now, walking across its hideous but expensive purple and red rug (personally selected by the chairman's wife, an aspiring decorator whose only client was her husband's corporation), she noticed the curtains twitch in the Human Relations Department's interior window which overlooked the company's reception area. There were rumors that Mr. Marks, the new CEO who had kicked his predecessor and one-time mentor upstairs to the chairman's office last year, had one of his flunkies monitoring the officers' comings and goings to determine who was taking long lunches or leaving early. Sally Ann was a mid-level corporate officer and so subject to scrutiny. Since she was returning from lunch on time, she turned to the curtained window and waved.

Getting off the elevator on her floor, Sally Ann noticed that the Legal Department was, as always, oppressively quiet. Luke Johnson, the general counsel—whose principal management theory was that 'people who like their jobs don't get sick'—discouraged any personal conversations lasting over 30 seconds by storming up and down the aisles between his employees' cubicles and glaring at the speakers until they returned to their corporate tasks. Everyone in the Legal Department lived in fear of triggering one of Luke's infamous temper explosions, during which he would scream incoherently, his face would turn purple and his temple veins would bulge almost to the bursting point.

One of Sally Ann's co-workers, an honors law graduate built like a red-haired female linebacker who scared all the men in the company, had once confided to Sally Ann that their boss intimidated her so much that she often felt like hiding under her desk. Sally Ann had kindly refrained from pointing out that her colleague's hefty torso was probably wider than the desk's kneehole.

Today Luke was nowhere in sight. Since it was Friday, Sally Ann hoped that he was drinking his lunch as he often did on the last day of the official work week. If so, Luke would get back late and be cheerful for the rest of the afternoon, thus giving Sally's stomach a chance to unknot as the weekend approached.

She soon noticed that the atmosphere in the Legal Department seemed even more gloomy than usual. Sally Ann walked over to Claudia, the head secretary, and asked, "What's going on?"

"Oh, Jesus," Claudia groaned, "Luke's on another rampage."

"What set him off this time?" Sally Ann asked. "I didn't do anything, did I?" She thought frantically about the projects she was working on. But since her general formula for avoiding Luke's wrath was to do meticulous work and keep her mouth shut, Sally Ann couldn't think of anything she might have screwed up. Not that Luke's tirades were restricted to employees who made mistakes, since he had a rotating shit list onto which everyone in the department eventually fell. Sally Ann had just gotten off the list, though, so she knew it was someone else's turn to be picked on for no reason.

"Luke and Paul had a big fight," Claudia said. "Last week Luke told Paul to draft a contract for one of the subsidiaries. Well, Paul gave Luke the first draft to review today and Luke hated it."

"What was wrong?" Sally Ann asked sarcastically. "Did Paul fail to address another issue that, according to Mr. I-graduated-from-Yale Law, is ultimately irrelevant but should have been considered anyhow?"

"Hell, I don't know," Claudia said. "But Luke was screaming so loud at Paul that the Xerox repairman quit working on the copier—he said he couldn't concentrate and he'd be back later in the afternoon."

"So where are Paul and Luke now?"

"Luke went stomping out about fifteen minutes ago. He said he was going to lunch. And Paul went rushing out of the department with his face all red—he's probably sitting in his car crying."

Since every employee in the Legal Department, from secretaries to attorneys, had at one time or another been reduced to tears of rage by the general counsel's unwarranted attacks, Sally Ann wasn't surprised. The females generally wept in the ladies' room with at least one other woman staffer standing by to hand out wads of Kleenex and reiterate what a shit Luke was. The men usually cried alone in their cars if they couldn't leave work for the nearest bar.

Karen, the Amazonian legal scholar, came out of the law library and joined Claudia and Sally Ann. "Were you around for the big scream-fest?" Sally Ann asked.

"I was hiding in the library. But I heard it all. Thank God it's Friday."

"Do you think we could plead justifiable homicide if we killed Luke?" Sally Ann said. "Or do you think that going to prison would be worse than working for him?"

"It's a toss-up," Karen answered. "At least it might be calm in prison and if the guards treated us as badly as Luke does we could file a civil rights lawsuit against the commonwealth."

"Your mother's a psychiatrist, right, Karen?" Claudia asked. "Could she get us some Thorazine to give Luke? I think he's beyond Prozac."

"You know, Mother told me once when I was on a diet that if I took too many Dexa-trim I'd get heart palpitations. We could put a whole package of those pills in Luke's coffee carafe. They might bring on a massive heart attack, as wired as he is most of the time."

"Well, there we are," Sally Ann said. "I can see it now—Luke writhing on the floor and us standing around counting down the seconds until brain damage sets in. Then we could call 911."

The three women snickered.

Karen added, "I described Luke's behavior to Mother a while ago—his roller-coaster mood swings, his temper, his obsessions. Mother said he could be schizophrenic or manic-depressive. Of course, she said he could also be JPC."

"What's JPC?" Claudia asked.

"Just plain crazy."

"I'm surprised one of the men hasn't punched out Luke, as nasty as he gets," Claudia said.

"Aside from the fact that they're weenies, I guess they hold back because they've got bills to pay like we do and can't leave in a blaze of glory," Karen replied. "What a way to go that would be, though. Luke would lip off one time too many and pow! there he'd be, flat on his back on the floor."

"We're really getting nasty," Sally Ann said. "Whatever shreds of decency we had left after law school have been trashed by working for Luke."

"Life's a bitch and so are we," Karen said. The women laughed and went back to their desks.

Can a Legal Flunky Find Key West?

Sitting in her work station, Sally Ann looked with distaste at the oatmeal linen partitions that divided her cubicle from Luke's on one side and Paul's on the other. Her company's renovated headquarters had won a number of architectural awards back in the 1980s for such innovations as eliminating private offices, and thus privacy, for all of its employees. Only the restrooms and one interview room in the Human Relations department were soundproofed; not even the CEO had the luxury of closing the door to his lavish office suite with its gleaming wood floors and wood-burning fireplace, since his office had no door.

Everything in the entire building, aside from the red and purple rug in the lobby's reception area, was beige, taupe or oatmeal; a person stepped from the elevators on each floor to be confronted by a vista of linen partitions, dreadful and overpriced modern art, and tropical plants. Had it not been for the differing plastic sculptures and shredded paper collages, Sally Ann, who had no sense of direction, would often have gotten lost in the building since each floor looked exactly the same as all the others.

Sally Ann did have a window, though. Some of her fellow drones were condemned to work in completely interior cubicles, the corporate equivalent of sensory deprivation tanks since they weren't allowed to hang anything on their partitions or have family photos or other mementoes on their desks—Mr. Marks was convinced that permitting employees to display personal memorabilia would destroy the aesthetic purity of the architects' design.

At least the company's headquarters was in Center City. Sally Ann had previously, and briefly, worked in another sterile modern building situated in an isolated Montgomery County office park. At lunch time there was no entertainment other than walking around the employees' parking lot and staring at the acres of trees and grass that surrounded the building like the waters around Alcatraz. Those employees still eating in the glass-walled corporate cafeteria would watch their co-workers pacing the parking lot like guards overseeing prisoners walking the yard.

God, I hate the suburbs, Sally Ann thought. Now I work where there are people and restaurants and stores. A little voice inside her added, yeah, and now you work for a psychopath.

Not for long, I hope, Sally Ann told herself. But until then, back to work.

She spent the remainder of the afternoon at her computer reviewing files, drafting memos, and writing letters. Sally Ann kept on top of her work but it was a never-ending flow of corporate dreck; she completed one file and another took its place. Generally there was little aside from Luke's tantrums and her menstrual cycle to distinguish one day from the next.

Occasionally to break the monotony Sally Ann would hand write phony memos and letters, which she never entered into her PC since it was widely believed that the company had installed monitoring software into its computer network. Using the gold-nibbed fountain pen that her husband had given her when she graduated from law school, she would write on a legal pad, "In response to your recent memo, I believe that the Marketing Department's proposal will subject this company to unlimited but well-founded liability," or "I have reviewed and, under my supervisor's duress, approved the specious and outrageously one-sided contract you recently sent me."

But once written, these documents were quickly torn up and thrown away. Sally Ann then returned to producing well thought out and legally sound analyses of issues about which she couldn't have cared less aside from her own pride in doing her job well.

Sally Ann had worked for her employer, which made component parts incorporated into heavy auto-manufacturing equipment, for three years. After leaving several unsatisfactory legal jobs since earning her law degree, she had started her current employment with an unwonted feeling of expectation. She liked and respected the two attorneys who headed the company's Legal Department and at first found her duties to be fairly interesting.

Sally Ann had easily mastered her job, though, and soon realized that the repetitive nature of the corporation's legal work bored her. However, she was fairly content for the first year since the general counsel and her second in command were genial people who ran a department where the work was done quickly and efficiently but in a pleasant and generally relaxed atmosphere.

On the strength of finally having a decent job, Sally Ann had even let her husband convince her that they should take out a second mortgage to finance a complete renovation of their old house, which they had been slowly remodeling on a piecemeal basis for years.

Two months later, the general counsel, a dignified African-American woman, had stunned everyone in the company by announcing that she was retiring and moving back home to Mobile. Sally Ann, who had never known anyone, either black or white, who had voluntarily set foot in Alabama, finally got up the courage to ask her why.

"I just turned 60," Mrs. Parker had said. "At my age, people want to reconnect with their roots. Besides, I'm sick of dealing with the cold Northern Ne— . . . blacks who fill this city."

Sally Ann hadn't dared to venture into the minefield of a racial discussion with her supervisor, although she couldn't resist saying, "But Alabama?"

"It's not that different from here, young lady," Mrs. Parker said. Then she had laughed and added, "Remember, in the last election, President Clinton's chief political adviser said that Pennsylvania consists of Philadelphia and Pittsburgh with Alabama in between."

Before she left, Mrs. Parker had recommended that her assistant counsel, a capable, intelligent man, be promoted to head the Legal Department. The Board of Directors, however, had refused to promote him since he hadn't attended a prestigious law school. The assistant counsel promptly took himself and his skills to a lower-paying government job in Washington; the company then hired Luke, a third-tier Ivy League graduate whose lack of competence was exceeded only by his insecurity and arrogance.

Sally Ann's job went from tolerable to awful within a matter of weeks. By the time she realized that the chaos and uproar into which her new boss had plunged the Legal Department were permanent, the city's major law firms and corporations were undergoing one of the huge shakeouts that periodically plague the legal world. Hundreds of attorneys were looking for non-existent jobs, and there was nowhere for her to go.

In the evenings, when she was at home in her exquisitely renovated house, Sally Ann thought that she could endure being trapped in her job by two mortgage payments. She would walk through her clean, sparsely-furnished house, admiring the few pieces of good furniture and the oil paintings she and her husband had bought in lieu of filling the house with less-expensive furnishings. She would enjoy the gleam of lamplight on the beautifully-refinished wood floors, which dully reflected the replastered, repainted walls and glowing woodwork. As she watered the large tropical plants which offset the sparseness of the furnishings, she would think with satisfaction that she had escaped the sad, shabby dullness of her parents' home.

During each workday, though, when she was far from the serene refuge of her house and had to confront the angry tension that now permeated the Legal Department, Sally Ann often thought that the price she was paying for her home was too high. She had even considered selling the house and moving somewhere smaller and cheaper, but two separate real estate appraisers had told Sally and her husband that, in the current sluggish real estate market of the mid-1990s in Philadelphia, they couldn't recover the cost of their renovations, no matter how beautiful the house was.

Sally Ann's telephone rang. "This is Sally Ann Stanton. How may I help you," she answered.

"Sally Ann," a male voice boomed in her ear. "This is Greg Owens in International. I need to find out the status of the management contract for our new Italian affiliate."

"I'm sorry, Greg, but I can't help you," Sally Ann said. "Luke is working on that contract himself and he usually doesn't discuss his files with the rest of us."

"Well, Sally Ann, I'd really appreciate it if you'd check with Luke and then get back to me," Greg said heartily.

"Certainly, Greg, I'd be happy to," Sally Ann answered, thinking that even the company's senior managers shrank from dealing with Luke and insulated themselves from direct contact with him whenever possible.

She wrote a brief note to Luke and walked around the partition to put it on his desk, since she knew he had never returned to the office after his fight with Paul. Although they sat only ten feet away from each other, Sally Ann and Luke seldom spoke. She generally addressed most of her comments to him in writing. Doing so enabled her to escape his frequent sullenness, blasts of withering sarcasm, and lengthy, stream-of-consciousness monologues which reminded her of a cable TV documentary she had once seen about Hitler and his flunkies at Berchtesgaden.

What a way to run a department, Sally Ann thought as she returned to her cubicle. She looked at the clock and saw that it was 5:00—time to start straightening up her desk.

The week finally over, Sally Ann drove home. She glanced at the Jimmy Buffett tape sticking out of her car's tape deck. "Well, Jimmy," Sally Ann said, "someday I'll find my own Key West, and unlike you, I'm going to stay in paradise when I get there."

A Piranha and a Proto-Slacker

On Sunday morning Sally Ann was swimming laps in the indoor pool at the local YMCA while her husband, Joe, and Bubba, their fat, elderly wire-haired terrier, snoozed blissfully at home. As usual on Sundays, clusters of elderly businessmen stood talking in the heated pool's shallow end, forcing the serious swimmers to dodge them as they turned after completing each lap.

Sally Ann finished her 40 laps and leaned back against the pool's wall while she caught her breath. She pulled down her goggles and floated her legs, relaxing in the warm water with her eyes closed.

"My, but you are looking particularly beautiful today," an admiring baritone voice with a heavy Middle Eastern accent said.

Sally Ann opened her eyes and peered nearsightedly at the man standing in the water next to her. "Hello, Ariyeh," she said politely, thinking, damn, I was hoping I'd miss this jerk.

"Why don't you let me take you to lunch," Ariyeh said, looking longingly at Sally Ann's breasts outlined through the thin wet fabric of her racing suit.

"Sure, Ariyeh. As long as the invitation includes my husband," Sally Ann answered.

"But Sally Ann," Ariyeh protested, "just this once can't you pretend you're single for a day and go out with me?"

"Nope," Sally Ann said coolly. "Sorry. But I'm sure that many of the ladies here would love to join you for lunch."

Ariyeh, a paunchy, heavily-bearded émigré from Israel, looked mournfully at the middle-aged female bodies splashing nearby. "Someday, Sally Ann, you will go out with me."

When the Pope converts to Islam, Sally Ann thought. "Only if my husband comes along," she said. "Otherwise, no." She added, "You know, there's a Jewish Community Centre not far from here— one of my colleagues has told me that they have a lot of programs for single people." She didn't add that her co-worker, Avery Weinstock, had told her that he was going to date every gentile woman he could before he was forced to settle down with one of the "frigid princesses," as he described them, who prowled the Singles Nights trolling for highly-paid surgeons and attorneys, leaving a trail of freezer-burned males in their wake. As only a staff lawyer in a corporate legal department, "my carats won't be big enough for any of those shrews," Avery had said sourly. Sally Ann had thought it best to change the subject.

"Your husband is a very lucky man," Ariyeh said. "To have married a beautiful girl who is also smart enough to be a lawyer."

"Yeah, and I can cook, too," Sally Ann said drily as she climbed out of the pool. "Well, I'm out of here, Ariyeh. Bye."

Sally Ann grabbed her towel and hurried off to the locker room, knowing that Ariyeh was staring lecherously at her backside as she walked away from him. The principal disadvantage to swimming at the Y on Sundays was the high proportion of elderly mashers who congregated there. Sally Ann couldn't wear her contacts while swimming and was too nearsighted to see the old goats coming until it was too late.

After showering and dressing, Sally Ann drove home. Joe and Bubba were waiting for her when she got home, both with the same 'where are the treats' look in their big brown eyes.

"Hi, guys," Sally Ann sang out as she stepped into the kitchen. Joe turned from the coffeemaker and smiled at her. Bubba ran up and sniffed the bag of doughnuts Sally Ann had bought on her way home.

"Hey, puppy," she said, rubbing his fat little body. "You almost didn't get your goodies this morning."

"Why's that?" Joe asked as he poured boiling water from the tea kettle into Sally Ann's teapot.

"Ariyeh the ex-Israeli paratrooper was at the pool. He kept asking me to go out to lunch with him."

"I see he didn't sweep you off your feet."

"More like he didn't pull my feet out and drag me under the water while he molested me."

"Maybe we'd better get you some prescription goggles so you can see these lechers in time to get away from them," Joe said.

"Thanks, sweetie. Why don't you come swimming with me and protect me?"

Joe put his arm around Sally Ann's waist and hugged her. "Because even though you look so thin and delicate you don't need protection any more than a piranha does. Besides, I'm saving my Sunday morning energy for sex."

"Well, in that case, the piranha will keep on fighting off the land sharks by herself," Sally Ann said, standing on her toes to kiss him on the cheek.

Sally Ann and Joe sat at the kitchen table, reading the Sunday newspaper and feeding bites of doughnut to Bubba. Sally Ann scanned the want ads; as usual, the few attorney listings were for entry-level positions for which she was completely over-qualified.

"I don't know how much longer I can keep on working for Luke," Sally Ann said. "He's getting worse all the time."

Joe laid down the sports page to pour himself more coffee. "Why the hell does your company put up with him?"

"I have no idea. He's rude to the company's clients, bullies its managers and terrorizes his staff," Sally Ann said gloomily. "Maybe he has compromising photos of Mr. Marks." She ate half a glazed doughnut and added, "I keep hoping he'll have a stroke during one of his screaming fits and we'll get rid of him that way."

Joe, who had thought Sally Ann was exaggerating the severity of Luke's mood swings and outbursts until the two men had played on opposing corporate softball teams the previous summer, said, "Look, if it gets bad enough and you still haven't found another job, just quit. If we cashed in your 401(k) we could pay off the second mortgage. Then we could get by on my salary."

"I don't want to do that," Sally Ann said. "Once we paid off the second and paid the IRS penalty for early withdrawal on the 401(k), nothing would be left in my retirement account." She drank some tea, then added, "But I might be forced into it. I've been getting chest pains at work that are so bad I can't breathe. The other day Karen got so upset that she actually broke out into hives."

"Jesus," Joe said. "You know, Sally Ann, since you got out of law school you've worked for some real assholes but Luke is definitely the worst."

"I've had a real run of bad luck, that's for sure. Or maybe it's not bad luck—maybe that's just how most lawyers are. I can't decide if jerks go to law school, or if law school turns ordinary people into pigs, but either way I'm sick of working with them."

She added, "In fact, I don't really know if I want to go on practicing law. I don't know if I want to do anything except lie on the sofa and read mysteries. I'm too old to be a slacker but that's what I've turned into."

"Maybe you're a proto-slacker," Joe said, smiling at her. "These feelings of yours aren't exactly new."

Sally Ann laughed, wondering how anyone could be married to a person with no sense of humor.

"Besides," Joe said, "you want to do more than just read and couch. Don't forget obsessively listening to Jimmy Buffett songs."

"Those days may be over. I was doing some research on Florida business trends for an analysis I'm writing at work, and I came across an interview with him."

"Uh oh," Joe said. "What's he done to betray your militant fandom?"

Sally Ann looked embarrassed. "Oh, the article said he's becoming a major player in the south Florida economy. The laid-back Caribbean cowboy has turned into a driven entrepreneur." She poured herself more tea and added indignantly, "I even found two articles about him in 'Forbes.' He used to get interviewed in 'Rolling Stone,' now he's talking to the conservative creeps who read business magazines."

"Are you going to spread the word to the rest of the Parrot Heads?" Joe asked teasingly. "Don't tell me . . . now that Jimmy's acknowledged that he's a man of means, guys in pin-striped suits wearing glasses and power ties are going to sell investment-tip T-shirts at his concerts?"

Sally Ann smiled unwillingly, then laughed at the thought of pale, weedy corporate types earnestly spouting financial maxims to the tanned, beer-drinking, grass-skirt and sharks' head wearing partiers who fervently attended all of Buffett's live performances.

"Besides, it's his life, Sally Ann. You can still listen to his music," Joe added.

"I guess," she said. "I just had this fantasy that maybe it really was possible to get off the treadmill and stay off it. You know, drinking pina coladas, lying in a hammock, ogling studmuffins for me, sandbunnies for you."

"You don't drink and you hate direct sunlight," Joe pointed out.

"Don't be so literal," Sally Ann snapped. "You know what I mean."

"Yeah, I know what you mean, baby. I have my own escape dreams. My life's fulfillment doesn't come from being an engineer, you know."

"I hope your plans include me," Sally Ann said.

"Always."

Sally Ann stood up and walked around the table. She stood behind Joe and put her arms around him. "Sorry I snapped at you."

"And so you should be. You traumatized Bubba, you wench," Joe said, laughing as he looked at the doughnut-stuffed dog sleeping at his feet.

"I can tell he's paralyzed from anxiety," Sally Ann said derisively. She leaned over and started kissing Joe's neck and shoulder. She slipped her hand down the front of his shirt and stroked his thick chest hair, feeling his nipples harden as she gently sucked the side of his neck. "How about taking me upstairs and making me forget my problems?"

"Before I've finished the sports page?"

"I'll make it worth your while," she said, kissing his right ear and sideburn.

Joe pushed back his chair and stood up. "I guess I'd rather make love with my wife than read about the Phillies losing their first three games of the season."

"I'm honored," Sally Ann said. "Choosing me over sports."

"Don't get conceited," Joe said, fondling her as they walked upstairs to the bedroom.

After they finished loving each other, Sally Ann floated in post-sex bliss as she lay by Joe's side in their big four-postered bed. She was so relaxed she felt as if her bones had dissolved.

Joe picked up the television remote and started scanning the channels. When he hit a country music program he stopped; "Who's the Blonde Stranger," an old Jimmy Buffett video about an unfaithful married couple's dalliances at the beach, was playing.

"We'll find our beach," Sally Ann murmured. "Except we'll go there together." She drifted off to sleep, pressed against Joe. He smiled and went back to channel-surfing.

Chapter Two

No Menopause, No Retirement

Working for Big Nurse

The Legal Department was effectively shut down; Sally Ann and her co-workers had nothing to do. In one of his periodic fits of paranoia, Luke Johnson had refused to delegate any files to his staff for the past three week. The work stacked up in his office as Luke fielded outraged calls from other department heads, all demanding to know what the hell was going on.

No one could simply bypass Luke and directly call Sally Ann or Paul or Karen to get their legal questions answered or their documents reviewed. Luke had informed every senior manager in the company that all inter-departmental correspondence was to come first to him. He had also told his staff that they couldn't give advice over the telephone with regard to any matter he hadn't first reviewed.

So Sally and Ann and the other lawyers sat in their cubicles, staring at the blank oatmeal linen padding while trying to look occupied. Paul and Greg were really playing computer games on their PCs while Avery read a copy of *Iron John* hidden in a legal advance sheet. Karen sat in the law library barricaded behind stacks of case reporters, eating peanut M&Ms and reading 'Sports Illustrated.'

Sally Ann worked on questions for Pop Culture Jeopardy, a game Joe and she played. She checked her watch. Only five minutes had passed since the last time she looked. Her day was moving so slowly it seemed that time had stopped.

Nineteen years of formal education (20 counting kindergarten), Sally Ann thought glumly, and I'm making up questions for a phony game show. The only thing worse than being at work on a busy day is sitting here with nothing to do.

"Goddammit, I'm swamped with work!" she heard Luke screaming at some hapless person who'd telephoned to ask why the Legal Department wasn't releasing any legal opinions. "No, I will not give the file to Sally Ann or Avery. I'm the lawyer handling this matter and that's final."

Sally Ann heard Luke slam down his phone. The soft-paneled side of her cubicle thudded as he threw the offending file against their shared partition.

She sighed, thinking, This department is a lunatic asylum and I am Randle Patrick McMurphy.

If I just quit, could I collect unemployment benefits to help pay the bills, she wondered. No. The fact that I work for a deranged Big Nurse disguised as the general counsel and he's slowly frying my brain without benefit of electrodes doesn't constitute the intolerable working conditions that justify walking away from a job. I'd tell the unemployment examiner that my boss is crazy and he or she would just shrug and say 'They all are.'

So, what are my options? she thought. I haven't been able to find another law job. Therefore, I can stay here until I do and maybe I won't lose my mind or have a heart attack. Or I can quit, lose all my retirement money, and be supported by my husband.

Not much of a choice. But maybe I could get a job doing something other than law. Like what? Sally Ann asked herself sardonically. I'm not qualified to do anything but be a lawyer. I went to law school because I wasn't trained to do anything at all when I got out of college.

She stared out her window. Were her life's alternatives limited to working for Luke or possibly living on a steam grate if Joe and she lost their house?

Cut it out, Sally Ann ordered herself. Quit feeling sorry for yourself. She breathed deeply. I know what I can do. I'll write a pop psychology book for the '90s: 'Self Pity Sucks: Stop Whining and Get On With Your Life.'

I'll never make it onto Oprah or Geraldo or Montel, though. How would they advertise the show: "Live at 4:00—Quiet Reserved Author Refuses to Promote Book or Discuss Self." "Well, Phil," I'd say, "I really feel that my book speaks for itself, and frankly, my personal joys and sorrows are private."

"But Sally Ann," Phil would say unctuously, "can't you at least tell me your book's central premise"

"Of course, Phil," I'd say. "My book's thesis is, Keep Your Pain to Yourself." At which point Phil would shrug helplessly, cut to a commercial, and I'd be hustled off the stage.

Sally Ann's telephone rang. "This is Luke," she heard her boss say into the receiver, his voice also drifting over the top of their partition. "Will you come into my office, please."

Oh, shit, Sally Ann thought. She stood up and walked around the partition into Luke's cubicle. His desk, credenza and visitors' chairs were stacked with files which spilled over onto the window ledge and the floor.

"What can I do for you, Luke," Sally Ann asked smoothly, mentally adding 'you asshole.'

Luke pulled a letter from the top of a huge stack of papers teetering at the edge of his desk. "The company has gotten another request for a contribution from the College of General Studies at Penn. I want to decline it. I don't know why the hell these people are asking us for money."

"Certainly, Luke," Sally Ann answered as she took the paper from Luke's hands. "Anything else I can help you out with?"

"No, no, things are pretty well under control. That will be all."

Sally Ann went back to her desk thinking that few things were more demoralizing than being prevented from using her professional skills when the need for them was so great. God save me from insecure control freaks, she thought.

Smiling uneasily, Sally Ann looked at the letter Luke had given her. She knew very well why the University of Pennsylvania kept requesting donations.

About a year ago Sally Ann had written one of her phony letters addressed to the Penn adult education department, asking if the university press would be interested in printing her monograph, "Nihilism and the City: A Countervailing Ethos in the Works of Jimmy Buffett." Her draft had gotten mixed up with an actual stack of letters Sally Ann was proofreading. One of the secretaries had typed it on company letterhead and then mailed it.

The University of Pennsylvania had declined to publish Sally Ann's non-existent article. However, since then Penn had been asking for money "on the basis of your corporation's demonstrated interest in the arts" and Sally Ann had been much more careful with her diversionary drafts.

Sally Ann dropped the letter in the middle of her empty desk and walked to the law library. "What's going on?" she asked Karen.

Karen laid down her 'Sports Illustrated' and answered, looking lustfully at the cover picture of a recently-retired football player, "If I get reincarnated I want to come back as that man's jockstrap."

"Still nursing your passion for over-the-hill athletes, I see," Sally Ann said as she sat down at the polished mahogany library table and propped her feet on the next chair. She tucked her skirt around her legs and wiggled her toes inside her polished leather pumps. "Most of those guys are really stupid, you know."

"Who cares?" Karen said. "I'm not interested in talking to them. Besides, this one was a quarterback. He'd have to have at least a minimal level of intelligence."

She added, "To go from the sublime to the ridiculous, what's Luke doing?"

"Telling anyone who calls or comes by that he's overwhelmed with work but everything's under control. This while files are spilling out over the top of our partition."

"That asshole," Karen said. "Bob Raymond from the Finance Department told me that three weeks ago he sent Luke the papers on a multi-million dollar line of credit the company's getting from one of the big banks. He said they can't lock in the interest rate until Luke okays the documents.

"In the three weeks Luke's been sitting on the file the rates have gone up so the company's going to have to pay hundreds of thousands of dollars in additional interest. Bob said he keeps calling Luke and asking him to give the file to one of us so they can close but Luke won't do it."

"I think Bob called again this afternoon," Sally Ann said. "Luke basically told him to go to hell and then threw the file against our partition."

"You know," Karen mused, "if a female manager acted as hysterically as Luke does the company would throw her out on her ass. But Luke they put up with."

"It's not just Luke," Sally Ann said. "Every place I've ever worked has had at least one male screamer who's tolerated and protected by the other men. But let a woman have one bad day and the guys call her a bitch and start campaigning to get rid of her." She added, "Right now I've got PMS so bad my nerves feel like a frayed rubber band. But I manage to be civil to everyone. If I can do it why the hell can't Luke?"

"Because he can get by with being a prick," Karen answered.

"Even if I could get by with it, I wouldn't take my moods out on other people," Sally Ann said. "It seems to me that the real bitches are usually men. In my entire professional life, the most emotional and irrational people I've had to deal with have all been male."

"By and large that's been true for me too. I have to say, though, that Luke is the biggest jerk I've run into . . . or even heard of, for that matter."

"The worst lawyer I've heard of is that creep Dickie Pete Hancock whose ads are plastered all over the subways. He beat up his female partner."

"Oh Jesus," Karen said. "How did you hear about it?"

"At a women's bar association meeting a few months ago. That clown is a cracker from a Florida trailer park who apparently hates women."

"So why did he go into business with a female?"

"I have no idea."

"Did the woman press charges?"

"I don't think so. You know how much of a boys' club the legal community here is. The story I heard is that she was afraid she'd get marked as a troublemaker if she called the police or filed a civil lawsuit against him. So she just left her business and is now working as a paralegal since she can't find another attorney's position."

"That really sucks," Karen said angrily. "I'll tell you something. If Luke ever hits me I'm going to Mr. Marks' office with a shopping cart and I'll tell him to fill it to the top with money."

"Luke wouldn't hit one of us. His idea of a worthy opponent is a 20-year-old pregnant secretary like Annie. Claudia told me that Luke got so mad at Annie yesterday it looked like he was going to smack her."

"And what was Annie's crime?"

"She changed the date on one of Luke's letters without asking him."

"Unbelievable."

The two women sat in a depressed silence. "I can't stand this," Sally Ann said. "It's 4:30—I'm going to the Twentieth Street Bar and Grill. Would you like to come?"

"I'd love to go with you," Karen said longingly. "But I'd better not. I've sneaked out early the last two afternoons." A sigh rippled through her large frame.

"This is worse than high school," Sally Ann said musingly. "Ditching work. What's next—hall passes to go to the bathroom?"

"Don't even think that. Luke would probably try it if the idea occurred to him."

"On that note," Sally Ann said, "I'm leaving. See you tomorrow."

"See you," Karen answered. "Enjoy your freedom while you can. We both know that in a few weeks or months Luke is going to start frantically passing out the files he's sitting on and then he'll be enraged if the department isn't back on track in two days."

"Maybe I'll have won the lottery by then and it won't matter."

Stepped on a Pop Tart

Sally Ann sat at a small table in the Twentieth Street Bar and Grill. She drank a cup of hot tea and ate several bites of flan, savoring the rich vanilla custard and the caramelized sugar glaze. She was finally starting to relax.

As usual, being at her favorite restaurant cheered her up. Aaron, her server, came up to the table. "Do you need anything else, Sally Ann?" he asked as he poured more hot water into her teapot.

"Just a lobotomy. It's been one of those days."

I hear you, sweetheart," Aaron said as he brushed crumbs from the tabletop. Just then a yell came from the nearby bar.

"What's going on?" Sally Ann asked.

"Four drunks are arguing over the words to a Jimmy Buffett song. They've played 'Margaritaville' six times on the jukebox and still can't decide if it goes 'stepped on a pop top' or 'stepped on a Pop Tart.'"

"'Stepped on a Pop Tart?' That doesn't make any sense."

"Tell me about it, sweetie. If I hear that damn song one more time I'm going to drop a pot of coffee on one of them."

"I think I can help you out," Sally Ann said as she pulled a copy of 'The Parrot Head Handbook' from her briefcase. "The words to 'Margaritaville' are printed on page 8. See, it clearly says 'stepped on a pop top.'

"Go ahead and show them the lyrics. But I want my book back," Sally Ann said as Aaron started to laugh.

"You, a Jimmy Buffett fan? I wouldn't have thought it." Aaron looked at her neat linen dress and double strand of pearls. "You have hidden depths, Sally Ann."

"So I've been told. I still want my book back," she called to the departing Aaron as he disappeared into the bar.

Sally Ann had forgiven Jimmy for his wealthy businessman status one night as she gloomily sorted through her CDs. She had every Buffett album ever recorded, except 'Rancho Deluxe,' on either tape or compact disc. She had decided, while looking at the laughing, mustached Jimmy Buffett pictured on the 'Floridays' cover, that anyone who once looked that good could be forgiven many transgressions. Sally Ann didn't usually find blond men attractive, but something about the 'Floridays' photograph drew her, probably the genial ease reflected in the singer's face. She even liked his open shirt and gold chain.

Taken in by a handsome face. I guess I'm getting shallow, she had thought. What the hell—everyone needs some shallows in their lives.

"Compliments of four drunken Parrot Heads, Sally Ann," Aaron said as he deposited the Handbook and a salt-rimmed margarita on her table. "You've also got an invitation to go to the Buffett concert in Cincinnati this summer.

"Some girls have all the luck," he added snippily. "Two of those guys are too butch for words."

"Don't be jealous, sweetie." Sally Ann put enough money to cover her tab plus a generous tip on the table. "You can have the margarita. I've got to get home to my husband."

She started to walk away, then stopped. "Oh my dear Lord," Sally Ann said, looking at a young girl who had just come in the front door. Her face powdered geisha-white, her short dyed black bob matched her black lipstick, black mini-dress and black stockings that ended several inches below the dress's hem, exposing the girl's white thighs. She wore black combat boots and the hand gripping her black plastic Betty Boop purse had black polish on its nails.

"Do I need to update my wardrobe, Aaron?"

"If you do, you'll sure be noticed at the next Board of Directors meeting."

"What a thought," Sally Ann said. "Most of those people think a pink shirt worn with a navy suit is too flashy."

"Corporate types—how dreary," Aaron said with a shudder. "I dated a yuppie once. He dressed like Ward Cleaver, and he was only 28."

"You two must have made an odd couple," Sally Ann said, looking at Aaron's handsome African-American face and noting the flair with which he wore his waiter's black T-shirt and black jeans.

"More than you can imagine, dear." Aaron picked up the money and started to clear Sally Ann's table. "You'd better get on home and do your June Cleaver routine, Sally Ann."

"Not tonight," she answered. "Tonight is Joe's night to cook, which means we'll be going out to dinner."

"Like I said, some girls have all the luck."

"See you, Aaron," Sally Ann said as she left the restaurant. She drove home to her husband and Bubba, thinking happily about both.

Lear and Present Danger

Stepping through the back door into her kitchen, Sally Ann punched the security code into the burglar alarm's keypad. There was a pile of dog poop in the middle of the floor; Bubba was nowhere in sight.

"Goddammit," she snapped, her good mood starting to fade. She stomped off to the bathroom to get some toilet paper and then cleaned up the mess.

The answering machine was beeping annoyingly. Sally Ann pushed the message button—Joe's apologetic voice spoke into the room. "Hey, babe, a client gave us some last-minute design changes and I have to re-work the specs. Don't think I'll make it home for dinner so go ahead and get something to eat. Sorry about this." The machine clicked off.

"Well this is just fucking perfect," Sally Ann said nastily as she stormed through the empty house. She went to the bedroom and changed her clothes, pulling on her loosest pair of sweats to ease the pressure on her aching breasts and abdomen. If my period doesn't start soon, I'm going to explode, she thought miserably.

The bedskirt twitched. Sally Ann saw the tip of Bubba's black nose and one paw stick out from under the edge of the embroidered linen. She dropped to her knees and looked under the bed.

"Okay, mister, what's your story?" She pulled Bubba out from his refuge. Sally Ann looked at his ashamed little face and said, "What's that? Your evil twin Joey pooped in the kitchen and then left, and now you have to take all the blame? Life isn't fair, is it kiddo." Bending over, she kissed the top of his warm furry head. "It's okay, baby—accidents happen even to the best of us."

Sally Ann put Bubba into the back yard while she decided what to do about dinner. "Tonight I'm eating a balanced meal from the four food groups—sugar, fat, chocolate and caffeine. To hell with the new food pyramid." She mixed up a batch of chocolate chip cookie dough, her panacea since her law school days, and put the cookies in the oven to bake.

Bubba scratched at the back door so Sally Ann let him in. He pranced eagerly into the kitchen, sniffing the warm cookie-scented air. "You're looking awfully perky," Sally Ann said. "Did the bad dog go out into the yard and now the good dog has come back in?

"Oh, quit slobbering," she added. "Don't you know it's degrading to beg? . . . Oh, you don't care if you're degraded as long as you get what you want?" She took a cookie off the wire cooling rack and picked the chips out of it, since Bubba, like all dogs, got violently ill if he ate chocolate. She gave the rest of the cookie to Bubba.

"What should we do tonight, sweetie?" Sally Ann asked her dog. "Daddy has to work late so it's just you and me. Oh, we can talk about it over dinner? Okay."

Bubba crunched down his dry dog food topped with chunks of last night's baked chicken as Sally Ann drank cups of hot tea and ate a dozen of her freshly-baked cookies. She had the kitchen Watchman turned on to the local news as she ate. "You know, Bubba," she said, "there should be one generic newscast and the anchors could just fill in the blanks each night, since the news is always the same—there are always drugs, murders and car wrecks.

"Thank God for the state news," she added, snickering over the latest update in the saga of the state senator hiding out in Martha's Vineyard to avoid being subpoenaed to testify in a Pennsylvania Supreme Court justice's impeachment trial. The senator's testimony was sought by the defense to buttress the indicted justice's claim that another judge had tried to run over him with his car in front of a Philadelphia luxury hotel. "And people say lawyers are venal but dull, Bubba," Sally Ann said. "Some of us are venal and amusing."

Sally Ann cleared her dishes from the table and put them in the dishwasher. "What should I do tonight, Bubba?" she asked her dog. "I've got PMS and I feel like shit . . . What's that? You think I should just go watch TV in bed and bag the whole evening? I totally agree. Thanks for talking things over with me."

Scanning the television listings, Sally Ann lay in bed with Bubba curled up next to her on top of the quilt. According to a typo in the Inquirer (Philadelphia, not National), 'Lear and Present Danger' started at 9:00. What an interesting movie that would be, she thought. Reagan, Goneril and Cordelia as three CIA ninja babes, Jack Ryan wandering the fields of Langley, Virginia, driven insane by using too much captured cocaine.

She saw that her favorite cop show was on and punched in the channel on the remote. The familiar opening montage of New York street scenes filled the television screen. The program had once been considered daring because its former male star had shown his naked backside in several episodes. To Sally Ann, though, the sight had been nothing to get excited about. "He needs to tighten up his glutes," she had told Karen the next day at work after she'd seen the man's slightly pendulous buttocks for the first time. "Now if he'd turned around, that might have been interesting."

"Fat chance," Karen had said. "Even in the movies there's no frontal nudity of any male I'd want to see. Have you ever noticed that? The men can slobber over a blonde screen goddess crossing her legs with no underwear on, but all we get is a middle-aged character actor's dickfest."

Sally Ann propped herself up on the pillows and watched her show. It was a repeat and her mind started to wander. A wave of hormone-induced melancholy washed over her.

She missed Joe. He was the only person she had ever let through the wall of her self-reliance, the only man on whom she'd ever taken a chance. When Sally Ann was seventeen she had decided, one night after seeing her father slapping her sick mother on the buttocks as her mother howled like an animal, that she would never love anyone again because the pain was too great. To keep her heart from rupturing from sorrow she had encased it in ice.

Her family wasn't close; their relationships were marked by emotional distance and festering, unspoken anger. Sally Ann and her sisters had been driven apart by the pain of their mother's recurring mental illness and their controlling father's emotional and then physical abuse of their mother.

Francis Fitzpatrick had died in the early '90s, after an eight-year physical decline that began after a coronary bypass operation and ended with him reduced to a whimpering child, senile and in diapers. Sally Ann's mother had remarried, much to her older sisters' chagrin. The fact that their new stepfather was kind and adored their mother, and gave her the loving marriage their father had denied her, didn't seem to matter to them.

Sally Ann loved her mother and was happy for her late-found good fortune. But her years as parent to her parents had taken their toll. Since she was fourteen Sally Ann had both mothered and fathered herself and her parents; in many ways she thought of her mother as her child. Her occasional requests for help from her sisters had been met with blame or indifference, so she had stopped asking.

There was only Joe in her life. They had met at St. Joseph's University, the Philadelphia Jesuit college that both attended even though Joe was a Methodist. They married after their sophomore year, when both were 20. Even now, fifteen years later, Sally Ann sometimes wondered uneasily if she had made a mistake by unthawing her heart and giving so much of herself to her husband. She always told herself that she hadn't erred—that even though it hurt she had to let herself love someone.

Sally Ann fell asleep and didn't hear Joe come home. He walked into the bedroom, loosening his tie with one hand and carrying the plate of cookies she'd left him in the other.

"These are great, honey," he said. Sally Ann didn't wake up. Joe walked over to the bed and looked at his sleeping wife and dog. Bubba half opened his eyes, growled faintly at Joe, and snuggled closer to Sally Ann.

Joe smiled at both of them. He would have liked to have had a child with Sally Ann but had to make do with their dog. Sally Ann had always been lukewarm to the idea of reproducing—having been brought up to believe that children in general, and she herself in particular, were burdens and nuisances, she'd never had any enthusiasm for the thought of having a baby. Her views had only hardened as time passed and her family's problems worsened. "People have children so they'll have someone to torture," Sally Ann often said bitterly after her years of helping to care for her parents. "I'll never do that to anyone."

So they had Bubba and not a kid. Most of the time Joe didn't really feel that there was a gap in his life. He worked such long hours that, when he was home, he wanted to spend time with his wife and not some screaming child. But occasionally a wave of sadness engulfed him when he let himself think about the daughter or son he didn't have, especially when his colleagues at work proudly showed photos of their offspring and talked about all their father-child activities.

Starting to doze off, Joe turned off the television and got into bed. He curled up behind Sally Ann and she pressed herself closer into his warmth, with Bubba plastered against her other side. Joe and the dog made a Sally sandwich, both of them comforted by the touch of the woman they loved.

Sally Ann woke up in the middle of the night with a case of killer cramps. Her period had started. She barely made it to the bathroom before she threw up. Her head was splitting and she couldn't stand without getting dizzy. She swallowed two of the prescription painkillers her doctor had given her and staggered back to bed. She wondered how many years she had left until menopause and retirement, the only two events she consistently anticipated.

I'm not going to work tomorrow, she told herself. Normally Sally Ann dragged herself to the office regardless of colds, flu or cramps, partly because Luke was so nasty to anyone who called in sick, and partly from her own sense of duty. Her only concession to the woes of female existence was trading menstrual horror stories with Karen in the ladies' room. Tonight, though, the unholy trinity of Luke, nothing to do, and physical pain had done her in; she couldn't face the thought of having to be civil and professional throughout another wasted day when she was too sick to stand up.

Fuck Luke, fuck my job, screw my family, fuck everything and everybody except Joe and Bubba. On that thought, Sally Ann fell asleep, amused despite her crabbiness and physical pain by the fact that both her husband and her dog were snoring in counterpoint.

Chapter Three

Edith Wharton Days

Eating Humble Pi

"And then, of course, the charities discovered my mother so we haven't had a minute's peace since then." The lawyer's smug face and his twitty little bow tie were irritating Sally Ann enormously. She buttered a roll and placed the knife on her bread plate.

"Is your mother in need of assistance?" she asked in an overly polite voice. The other attorneys at the table smothered grins.

"Of course not," Dan Geist snapped, his face turning red with annoyance. "The charities are asking my mother for contributions and inviting her to all of their events.

"By the way, that's my bread plate you're using," he added nastily.

"I don't think so," Sally Ann said coldly. "Drinking utensils go to the right of the main plate, bread and salad plates go to the left. This plate is on my left and it's my plate for the duration of this meal."

Geist glanced quickly around the table, looking to see if the other lawyers were using the bread plates on their right or left. Everyone was using the plate to his or her left. The man glared venomously at Sally Ann but shut up.

She sighed inwardly. It was going to be a long afternoon, putting up with this twerp and his condescension and his constant attempts to impress her with his alleged social standing. If you really come from a moneyed background, she thought, why didn't your parents get your teeth straightened and why did you go to Michigan instead of an Ivy League law school?

Sally Ann finished her chicken salad and looked around the dining room of the expensive club where they were having lunch. The other diners were predominantly male and middle-aged, with a scattering of women and toadying younger men. The only blacks and Latinos in the room were serving or busing the tables. Her table's elderly black waiter, dignified in his white jacket, began clearing their dishes, then asked for dessert orders.

Sally Ann was in Chicago. As Karen and she had feared, Luke had ended the Legal Department's two-month work drought by frantically dumping all of the withheld files on his staff. On two days' notice, Sally Ann had been sent out of town to handle an arbitration hearing in a contract dispute of which she'd been completely unaware until Luke tossed the plane ticket on her desk.

Dan Geist was the lead attorney for the other corporation involved in the arbitration. He was a principal in an expensive and prestigious 300-partner Chicago law firm which had such stringent internal security that its personnel needed electronic passes to go from one section of the firm to another.

Sally Ann had been given the tour that morning. She had seen the two-story atrium in the law library designed by a nationally-famous architect, the enormous computer center, the marble-floored conference wing with its five enormous meeting rooms, each served by uniformed maids who poured coffee and tea and distributed freshly-baked pastries to the pin-striped occupants sitting at the huge, circular, polished malachite tables. She had hung her coat in the North conference room's enormous walk-in coat closet, also marble-floored, and seen the endless row of khaki trench coats hung in a straight line to infinity.

Instead of being impressed, Sally Ann had thought, this place is beyond satire. She had noticed that, unlike the public spaces, Geist's office was the size of a utility closet, overpowered by the huge and ugly glass and wood table he used in lieu of a desk. Geist had told her that he had only recently joined his firm, having previously been with a "small, intimate" (150-partner) law firm that had disbanded. "And how many lawyers are in your department?" he had asked patronizingly. "I so seldom deal with in-house counsel."

Unfortunately, Sally Ann had thought, I so frequently deal with self-impressed jerks.

Sally Ann looked up from her dessert plate to see Geist's eyes fixed on her. He had been nattering on about a concert his wife and he had attended and she had tuned him out. "Excuse me, did you say something?" she asked.

"I said that the pianist began his recital by playing all of the Chopin preludes by memory. Are you familiar with the preludes, Ms. Stanton?"

Sally Ann, who had taken fourteen years of piano lessons, replied, "Yes. I can play about half of the preludes although I don't have them memorized, unfortunately. Did you know that Chopin modeled these pieces on the Bach preludes? Like the Bach works, the Chopin pieces are written in a musical progression to follow the 'circle of fifths' in which each piece's key matches the next note on the circle."

Geist stared at her blankly.

"Something I find really interesting, though," she continued, "is that apparently there's a point about two-thirds of the way through each Bach prelude that corresponds to the mathematical concept of pi. A friend of mine who has a doctorate in music education was telling me that mathematicians did a computer analysis of the preludes and found the correlation. I had always heard that math jocks really like Bach—I guess there's a reason for it.

"So, how was the rest of the recital, Mr. Geist?"

Dan Geist was so dumbfounded he couldn't think of another putdown. He changed the subject and started bragging about his acquaintance with attorney-novelist Scott Turow who also lived in Chicago.

"I don't think Turow's last few books have been as good as his *Presumed Innocent* or *The Burden of Proof*," Sally Ann said. "What's your opinion, Mr. Geist?"

Geist flushed and had to admit he hadn't read any of Turow's novels. Sally Ann smiled. She ate her crème brulee and drank her tea as the three other lawyers at her table chatted politely over their desserts and Geist sulked.

A kindly-faced older man at the next table was happily telling his companions about a recent Four Freshmen reunion concert he'd attended. Sally Ann mentally pictured a crowd of aging Republicans in madras golf trousers or headbands and pearls listening blissfully to the songs of their youth. Apparently the Four Freshmen had taken requests from the crowd. She imagined herself at the concert, demurely dressed in tasteful suburban clothing, asking for a four-part rendition of Jimmy Buffett's 'My Head Hurts, My Feet Stink, and I Don't Love Jesus.'

Lunch was finally over. The five attorneys returned to Geist's law firm located in a huge granite and glass skyscraper on Wacker Avenue. The two lawyers who had been brought along solely for intimidation purposes returned to their offices. Geist, his young associate/flunky, and Sally Ann went back to the North conference room. The three members of the arbitration panel were already there, sitting in their shirt sleeves and comparing their travel schedules for the next few months. The lawyers greeted the arbitrators and gave their business cards to the court reporter who had been hired to make a transcript of the proceeding.

As is customary in commercial arbitrations, there were three members of the panel, one chosen by Sally Ann's company, one by Geist's client, and a third, the "neutral," selected by the two partisan arbitrators. All three were men in their 60s, retired corporate executives who now worked the arbitration circuit.

"Are we ready to begin this hearing?" the neutral arbitrator, who acted as senior panel member, asked. "If so, as representative of the petitioner, will you please begin, Ms. Stanton."

"Thank you, gentlemen," Sally Ann said. "As set forth in our initial Statement of Claim, and as the previous months of discovery have shown, it is our position that because of changed circumstances the contract in question between my company and Mr. Geist's client puts us in a commercially untenable position. For this reason we feel that the contract should be abrogated or, at the least, substantially modified. Our reasons for saying this are as follows . . . ."

Sally Ann continued with her presentation, answering questions as they were posed by the panel. In the two days Luke had given her to prepare she had frantically studied the 3000 pages of deposition transcripts, the initial Statement of Claim and all other filings made by Luke in the case so that she could make an intelligent, reasoned statement at the hearing although she really wanted to tell Luke to stick the file up his ass.

After Sally Ann finished, Geist began his statement. Sally Ann had to admit that the man was a good lawyer although personally he was a pompous twit. He presented his client's position quietly, logically and without grandstanding. Thank God for small favors, Sally Ann thought.

The afternoon progressed. The hearing finished on time. "Well, Ms. Stanton and Mr. Geist," the senior arbitrator said. "Thank you for your statements. The other panel members and I expect to have reached our decision by a week from today.

"Unfortunately, due to our travel schedules, we can't return to Chicago for awhile. For this reason, we can either arrange a conference call next Thursday to tell you what we've decided, or we can all meet at the hotel in New Orleans where we're scheduled to be until the end of next week.

"What is your preference, Ms. Stanton?"

"It's likely that my general counsel, Mr. Johnson, will be the attorney who receives your findings, gentlemen," Sally Ann said. "Mr. Johnson has already advised me that he wants the panel's decision to be given in person, so we would prefer to come to New Orleans." Sally Ann didn't add that Luke always hogged the chance to travel anyplace interesting at the company's expense and would be furious if she turned down a chance for him to score expense account meals at the best New Orleans restaurants.

"And you, Mr. Geist?" the arbitrator asked.

"New Orleans will be acceptable to my client," he answered.

I just bet it's even more acceptable to you, sweetie, Sally Ann thought. Now you can bill your client for a whole day in New Orleans plus travel time and expenses, instead of settling for a fifteen-minute conference call.

"Then we'll meet again next Thursday in New Orleans. My secretary will fax both of you the hotel name and address, and the meeting time." The three arbitrators stood to indicate that the session was finished. Everyone shook hands and left the conference room.

Sally Ann stepped into the enormous closet and panicked slightly. She had forgotten in which quadrant she'd hung her trench coat and there were easily 200 other khaki coats hanging in the room. Oh, jeez, she thought, how can I find my coat without going through the pockets of everyone else's and looking like a thief?

She walked slowly down the endless tan line until finally she saw the corner of a familiar silk scarf sticking out of a pocket. She had found her trench coat.

"Good night, Ms. Stanton," the conference floor receptionist said from behind her enormous rosewood counter. "Good night," Sally Ann answered, trying not to slip on the marble floor in her high heels as she walked to the elevators.

Support staff and partners senior enough to go home at 5:30 crowded onto the elevator as it stopped at every floor. For each person who got on, there were at least five who had to wait for the next car. At every floor, each of which had its own lavish waiting area and receptionist, Sally Ann saw marble, heavy dark paneling and expensive, original artworks. She tried to imagine the monthly billing foundation that supported this overblown legal structure. She knew that behind the scenes young associate lawyers and junior partners were working slaves' hours and sometimes pulling all-nighters to run up the bills charged to the clients who ultimately paid for everything.

The elevator stopped again. Two young lawyers crowded on. "Why are you going home so early, Fitzgerald?" one young man asked the other.

"My wife had a kid this morning. I'm not going home, I'm going to the hospital to see them. I'll be back in a couple of hours," Fitzgerald answered. "My supervising partner doesn't know; I told my assistant to tell anyone who's looking for me that I'm working on a brief and can't be disturbed."

"You won't make partner cutting out early like this," the first man said, twitching his bow tie self-importantly. Fitzgerald didn't answer, or ask why the other man was leaving.

Junior, don't find out too late that you've sold out your wife and child for your hopes of a fancy house and a huge investment portfolio, Sally Ann thought. Get out of here while you have a chance. She looked at Fitzgerald's tired, drawn face and knew that, as awful as it was to work for Luke, she could never stomach being an attorney in a big private firm, gouging clients with inflated bills and competing with her cut-throat peers to advance to a senior partner's lavish office and salary.

She stepped from the elevator into the enormous beige marble lobby which was completely empty aside from the security desk and a huge abstract bronze sculpture hanging from the ceiling. There wasn't a chair, bench or even ledge on which a person could sit or lean, nor were there any plants, trees or flowers. All of the expensively dressed people crossing the empty stone floor or waiting by the banks of elevators with their polished metal doors seemed foreshortened and diminished by the huge empty space. Sally Ann thought that the architects' intent had been to convey a sense of the power and intimidation of the building's occupants, most of which were law firms. She found it too theatrical and over the top to be anything but cold and ugly, and had only listened politely that morning as Dan Geist blathered on about how imposing he thought it was.

Stepping out onto the street she hailed a cab. "O'Hare Airport, please," she said to the driver. Sally Ann enjoyed visiting Chicago, partly because its politics were as corrupt as those of Philadelphia. She remembered the FBI's Greylord judicial sting of the mid-'80s, a time when bent Chicago judges reportedly kept MasterCard machines on their desks as a convenience for those giving them bribes. She would have enjoyed asking her driver about the latest episodes in the Chicago saga, particularly about a tabloid headline she'd seen that morning: "Cop Holds 'Old Lady in Ninja Outfit' at Gunpoint— 'I Didn't Know She Was a Nun,' He Said."

Since the driver barely spoke English, though, they rode in silence to the airport. Sally Ann gritted her teeth as the cabbie ran red lights, cut off other drivers and slammed around corners. She wondered if Chicago, like every other city in which she'd ever ridden in a cab, made applicants for chauffeurs' licenses pass bad-driving courses.

They managed to get from the Chicago Loop to the Eisenhower Expressway without crashing the cab or killing any pedestrians. The driver careened down the freeway, weaving in and out of traffic, wailing Middle Eastern music playing on his tape deck. The cab's shocks were non-existent; Sally Ann bounced up and down in the back seat and wondered if the wheels were going to fall off. She began to regret not telling Joe and Bubba she loved them before she left home for her premature death in a Chicago cab.

Finally they reached O'Hare. The cab driver raced up the ramp to the departing flights area, slowing marginally as he almost hit an AVIS courtesy van. "What airline, madam?" the driver asked in barely understandable English.

"U. S. Air," Sally Ann squeaked, amazed that her vocal cords still worked.

Forced by traffic to slow down, the driver began muttering what Sally Ann assumed were Arabic curses. He continually honked his horn at every other vehicle until finally they reached the U. S. Air terminal. She paid the fare, noticing the driver's Star of David pendant and deciding that he must be an Israeli rather than an Arab, then walked weakly into the terminal. Why do I always run into the weirdos from Israel? she asked herself, thinking of Ariyeh and their last encounter at the Y swimming pool which had ended with her grasping his upper arm so hard her fingernails cut into his skin while she told him, quietly and pleasantly, how she'd mutilate him if he ever tried to grab her under the water again.

Her flight back to Philadelphia was timely by O'Hare standards— the pilot only had to wait 45 minutes past the scheduled departure time until the tower cleared him for takeoff. No one sat next to Sally Ann so she was spared having to make conversation with a total stranger. She fell into her usual airflight-induced state of relaxation— 30,000 feet in the air where neither her boss nor any other legal creeps could get to her.

Sally Ann wondered what it would be like to feel relaxed all the time. She resolved again that she was going to find some way to get the lawyers out of her life.

She picked up her copy of Edith Wharton's *Summer*, a novella she had started reading on her morning's flight. Sally Ann felt a sneaking sympathy for Mr. Royall, the book's aging, alcoholic attorney whose life was rotting away in a small town as he drank to forget his isolation and loneliness. I will not become a female Lawyer Royall, she told herself fiercely. I will not waste my life working for Luke.

A Do-It-Herself Vasectomy

The next morning, Sally Ann strolled into the Legal Department, ready to brief Luke on the arbitration hearing in Chicago. Luke wasn't in, though, and his cubicle appeared unoccupied.

"Where's Luke?" Sally Ann asked Claudia, the only person in the department privy to the general counsel's schedule.

"His wife had a baby this morning," Claudia answered.

"Excuse me?" Sally Ann said. "I didn't even know she was pregnant. I just love the open communication and warm intimacy in this department."

"Tell me about it," Claudia answered. "I didn't find out about the pregnancy until last week."

"So what is this kid?" Sally Ann asked. "Number three?"

"No. Number four—two by the first wife, two by the second."

"I can't believe there are two women on this earth who were willing to marry Luke," Sally Ann said. "It makes my skin crawl to think of anyone actually having sex with him."

"I know what you mean," Claudia said, shuddering. "He's always bragging to me about what a stud he is and how often he and his wife do it. All I can think of is a couple of dogs humping."

"My dog would be insulted by a comparison to Luke," Sally Ann said, laughing. "Besides, in Luke's case, he's probably a talker, not a doer."

She added, "Um . . . , to completely change the subject, I've noticed for several weeks that the secretaries seem to be avoiding me. Have I done something to offend someone?"

Claudia looked embarrassed. She said, not meeting Sally Ann's eyes, "Do you remember several weeks ago when Annie was in your office telling you about her baby shower?"

"Yeah. Did I hurt her feelings or something?"

"Oh no. Nobody's mad at you. But Luke got pissed off and came stomping out to my desk. He said I had to tell Annie and the other girls that from now on they can only talk to you about business matters."

"That . . ." Sally Ann choked back 'bastard' since she didn't swear in front of the staff.

"You know it drives him crazy that you won't talk to him, Sally Ann. He's always asking me, 'Why won't she come in my office? Why does she write me notes? Why can't she just talk to me?'"

"Because, like everyone else in this department, I hate his guts," Sally Ann snapped angrily and unthinkingly. "Besides, I told him flat out a few months ago why I keep my distance. He'd asked me why I avoided him and I said, 'Because you treat people badly, Luke. I keep you at arm's length so that we can continue to have a professional working relationship.'"

"Jeez, you have backbone," Claudia said admiringly. "Your message didn't sink in, though."

"What do I have to do to get through to that moron?" Sally Ann asked. "Smack him in the face with a board?"

"It's hopeless, Sally Ann. His ego blocks his brain from processing negative information . . . Besides, he's hot for you."

"Did he tell you that?" Sally Ann asked in outrage.

"No, but it's obvious. He's jealous of anyone who talks to you or who you pay attention to.

"You know," Claudia continued, "when we moved from the fourth floor Luke insisted that the architects put your cubicle next to his when they drew up the plans. That was the only thing he really demanded—that you sit next to him."

"Well, my day is shot to hell," Sally Ann said morosely. "And I was actually in a semi-good mood when I came to work.

"But I still have to talk to Luke about the arbitration. Will he be in at all today, or is he going to take the day off to celebrate his new demon spawn?"

Claudia laughed. "Shame on you, making fun of a little baby. To answer your question, Luke will be here later this morning for a few hours. Then he's leaving for a conference in Seattle—he'll be out of the office all next week."

"Well that's just great," Sally Ann snapped. "Luke organizes the department so that only he can make decisions, and then he doesn't bother to let his staff know when he's not going to be here. You'd better let the other lawyers know Luke's going to be out next week so they can clear any pending matters with him."

Sally Ann turned away from Claudia and walked slowly down the hall of padded beige partitions until she got to her cubicle. She dropped her purse and briefcase behind her desk and sat fuming in her padded beige swivel chair. So Luke didn't want the secretaries talking to her? So he was going to blow off his wife and new kid, as well as his entire staff, and go to a conference? So he had the hots for her? So what else could go wrong?

"So we didn't get my wife to the hospital in time to prep her for the delivery," Luke said to Sally Ann after she had hypocritically congratulated him on his new child later that morning. "The nurses stuck her in a delivery room and grabbed the first doctor who walked down the hall to deliver our kid.

"When the baby was coming out my wife lost control of her bowels and crapped on the doctor. He turned to me and said, 'This is why I'm a plastic surgeon and not an obstetrician.'" Luke laughed.

Sally Ann stared at him, flabbergasted. Luke and she didn't usually exchange ten words a month, but he had decided to volunteer this embarrassing story after she'd made a polite comment about his new child. You pig, she thought. Your wife ought to give you a do-it-herself vasectomy for talking about her that way.

She looked steadily at Luke without saying anything until his face and the bald spot that showed through his mousy brown hair turned red. He hastily changed the subject. "Well, tell me about the arbitration hearing."

"I think it went fairly well," Sally Ann said, "but, as you know, there are some fairly strong cases supporting the other side's position."

"Yeah, I know," Luke answered. "That's why I went with a private arbitration instead of filing a lawsuit—we're more likely to get a compromise ruling that's at least partly favorable to us. The arbitrators usually try to give something to each side instead of ruling completely in favor of one party and completely against the other."

Sally Ann refrained from pointing out that the contract in question had an arbitration clause requiring all disputes to be submitted to a panel of arbitrators instead of to the courts, a fact of which Luke was well aware. She briefed her boss on the hearing, letting him know the questions the arbitrators had raised and the points Geist and she had scored at each other's expense.

"So that's how the hearing went," she concluded. "The arbitrators can't go back to Chicago next week; they asked if we'd rather have them announce their decision by conference call, or whether we wanted to go to New Orleans and get the ruling in person.

"I didn't realize you're going to be in Seattle so I said you'd go to New Orleans. Do you want me to call Geist and see if he can get the arbitrators to reschedule?"

"No," Luke said. "I'm going to be really tied up the next few weeks."

Not with your wife and kids, I bet, Sally Ann thought sarcastically.

"You go ahead and go to New Orleans for me. Claudia can give you the number of my hotel in Seattle and you can let me know what the panel decided. Okay?"

"Okay," Sally Ann said. "Since the meeting's on Thursday, I'll probably take a day of vacation on Friday if that's all right with you." To Luke, vacation time was only a notch above sick days; his staff usually had to grovel for his permission to take any of the three weeks' vacation the company gave its officers. She added, "I'll pick up the tab for any non-business time I spend in New Orleans."

"Yeah, fine," Luke said distractedly, to Sally Ann's surprise. She had been expecting at least one snide comment about her proposed absence. "Well, I guess that will be all for now, Sally Ann."

"All right. Enjoy your trip to Seattle," Sally Ann said politely as she left Luke's office. Karen was waiting outside his cubicle, holding several files she needed to discuss with Luke before he left. Sally Ann knew that after Karen left, Avery, Greg and Paul would separately come to see Luke to get decisions about matters that, by Luke's decree, only Luke could decide. Had Claudia not told the staff about Luke's pending absence, the Legal Department would have come to another halt next week. What a way to run a department, Sally Ann thought for the millionth time, rolling her eyes as she passed Karen. She saw that Karen was wearing the blue and white ensemble that Avery referred to as her Israeli flag dress because of its size and resemblance to that country's national banner.

Sally Ann grinned and went back to her office, her mood starting to lift as she realized that Luke would be out of her life for a whole week and she was also getting a company-financed trip to New Orleans. She picked up her phone and called Joe at work. "Hey, hot stuff," she said, "how'd you like to go with me to the Big Easy next week?"

Proust Never Ate Stale Doughnuts

After Luke had finished his meetings and left the office, Sally Ann strolled down the hall and into Karen's cubicle. Aside from difficult childhoods and a shared distaste for the general counsel, the two of them had nothing in common. Sally Ann knew that Karen viewed her as a rival and was intimidated by her. She also knew that, as much as Karen griped about Luke, she badly wanted to get ahead in the Legal Department, envisioning herself as general counsel someday or, at least, as Luke's designated heir.

They had an uneasy alliance, though, arising principally from the fact that both were women working in a conservative, male-dominated corporation. They talked to each other because there was no one else to turn to when the loneliness of being among the few women in positions of authority became overwhelming, and also because each woman had a dry sense of humor that she had to keep hidden from the corporate men who were intimidated or irritated by the two women's relatively high status within the company's hierarchy.

"Did you know Luke's wife had a baby this morning?" Sally Ann asked as she sat down in one of Karen's beige upholstered visitor's chairs.

"Claudia told me about it," Karen answered. "So I congratulated Luke about the kid. He was actually civil for once—he said that his wife and he were glad the baby's a girl since now their family's balanced with two boys and two girls."

"Amazing," Sally Ann said. "When I mentioned the baby, Luke told me about how his wife got to the hospital late and crapped on the doctor who delivered the child."

"What do you mean, 'crapped on,'" Karen asked. "She yelled at him or something?"

"No, I mean defecated."

"He actually told you that?" Karen said incredulously. "I didn't think that even Luke would be that tacky."

"Well, he is and he did," Sally Ann said. "I was really embarrassed."

"I guess so," Karen replied. "I'd kill my husband if he ever told anyone a story like that about me."

"On the grossness scale, this beats the time Luke imitated a Great Dane relieving itself while I was in his office," Sally Ann said. "He really seems to have an anal fixation. And he wonders why I write him notes instead of talking to him."

"He's sure made some completely out-of-line comments to you," Karen said. "My most embarrassing corporate moment was once, during a meeting break where I was the only woman in the room, several of the men 'forgot' I was there and started talking about their prostates. I think your baby story beats that, though."

"You know," Sally Ann said, "when I was in law school some of the men in my class used to write obscenities on the walls about the females. Things like 'women law students are pigs and whores.' I thought that once we got out of school and established ourselves, that kind of crap would stop. But I guess it never does."

"When I was in law school," Karen said musingly, "another woman and I were talking to our torts professor after class. He looked at me and said, just out of the blue, 'You know, Ms. Brennan, we really need to get all you intelligent women out of this law school.'

"'Why is that, Professor?'" I asked him.

"'Because, Ms. Brennan,' he said pompously, 'all our best breeding stock is being taken off the market.'"

"How charming," Sally Ann said acidly. "What did you do?"

"I couldn't think of a good comeback so I just looked at him. The woman standing next to me, though, was one of my class's more militant feminists. She came close to having a stroke on the spot."

"And is this jerk still teaching?"

"Probably. I found out later that, despite his wife and four children, he'd had affairs with a number of his female students over the years. I guess he'd decided to be the high-IQ bull who would hopefully fertilize the smart cows."

"Unbelievable," Sally Ann said. "Speaking of fertilize, my criminal procedure professor brought his wife to the law school when she was in labor with their second kid. He was scheduled to give a lecture that afternoon and apparently thought that the world would end if he didn't go ahead and spout off on the Fourth Amendment.

"So he left his wife alone in his office, timing her contractions, while he went to his classroom and lectured us about search warrants."

"Did she drop the kid right there in the law school?" Karen asked.

"No. They made it to the hospital after class was over. But the dean got really mad and chewed out the guy."

"How did the dean find out about it?"

"He heard the woman groaning and went to investigate. I heard he got close to hysterical when he found his colleague's wife sitting, alone and in hard labor, in the man's office while her husband blathered through a routine lecture."

"My God."

"You know," Sally Ann said, her voice wry, "Proust thought about his past and was inspired to write a series of classic novels. I think about my past and all I get is a stomach ache."

Karen laughed. "I don't think that remembering the stale doughnuts and bad coffee from the law school vending machines has quite the emotional impact of Proust's tea and madeleines. Not, of course, that I've ever actually read any of his books."

"Neither have I," Sally Ann said. "As one of the Jesuits at St. Joe's used to say, a classic is a book everyone quotes but no one reads."

"To change the subject completely," Karen said, "should we have a 'Luke's Gone' party next week? We could have a pot-luck lunch with everyone in the department bringing something."

"Sounds good to me," Sally Ann said. "I'd be happy to bake some cookies or make a cake. The only thing is, Luke's sending me to New Orleans Wednesday night so the party will need to be Monday or Tuesday."

"That's what I was thinking of anyway," Karen replied. "I'll stroll around the department and see if enough people are interested and what they can bring. We can set everything up in the law library like we did for the non-Secretaries Day party when Luke was gone in April."

"This is so pathetic," Sally Ann said. "In every other department of this company the supervisors get along with their people, they all have lunch together once in a while, and they celebrate special events. Here we have to sneak around like terrorists if we all want to get together."

"Well, after Christmas last year, I'm never going to try to organize anything directly again," Karen said. "I learned my lesson."

"God, that was a fiasco," Sally Ann said as her neck muscles knotted at the memory. Karen and Sally Ann had set up a departmental Christmas luncheon at a Center City restaurant since Luke flatly refused to do anything at all for his much-abused clerical staff. ("They get their salaries, don't they?" he'd said to Sally Ann while adjusting the French cuffs of his bespoke shirt. "Why should they expect anything else?")

Karen had invited Luke to come along and he had rudely said no, although he'd given grudging permission for the luncheon to proceed. But he had been waiting for them when they got back, his face swollen and red with fury. He had ordered all five lawyers to sit in the library where he had raged and screamed incoherently at them for at least fifteen minutes while they sat in stunned silence. Sally Ann had walked out when Luke threatened to fire each of his attorneys for their alleged conspiracy to make him look bad. She had run to the ladies' room and thrown up, spewing out her lunch and her rage into the toilet.

She had come very close to quitting on the spot, just walking out and never coming back. She had been stopped only by the thought of her two mortgage payments and her fear of ruining Joe's Christmas.

There had been a few consequences of Luke's emotional beating of his staff, though. Before the Christmas luncheon, Sally Ann's dislike for Luke had been tempered by her recognition of his desperate insecurity. Since then she had lost all respect for him regardless of his personal problems. Further, her employment by the company was now only a short-term way to help pay the bills until she figured out what to do with the rest of her professional life.

"Then remember how annoyed Mr. Marks was when the Legal Department wouldn't gather with the rest of the officers around the Christmas tree in the atrium and sing Christmas carols?" Karen asked. "And how his assistant told him that she'd seen you crying and throwing up in the bathroom? He really reamed Luke for that one."

"Not that it had any lasting effect," Sally Ann said sourly, still embarrassed that others in the company had learned of her loss of control, "especially after Luke regained the high ground by telling Mr. Marks that he'd violated the anti-religious discrimination laws by making everyone sing Christmas songs." She stood up. "Well, I'd better get back to work. Let me know if the party's on and what I can bring."

"Ooh, food," Karen giggled as she walked out from behind her desk. "I am so compulsively oral. Just thinking about all those goodies next week makes me starving. I'm going to go buy some M&Ms from the vending machines."

Sally Ann watched as Karen's large, flag-swathed body lumbered toward the elevators. Clearly 'once through the lips, forever on the hips' was not her motto. She had always been a big woman but, since the birth of her second child, had gotten enormous. At a recent staff meeting Karen had announced that for years her wealthy psychiatrist mother had been raising hogs on her Midwestern investment farm. No one had dared to respond.

I've gotten lactose-intolerant when it comes to the milk of human kindness, Sally Ann thought, slightly ashamed of herself. She remembered that once, in a low moment, Karen had confided to her that her weight problems had started when she was a child and had overheard her recently-divorced mother telling a friend that she would gladly give her children away if it would make their father come back.

After sitting down at her desk, Sally Ann looked at her watch. Three more hours until 5:00 p.m. and the start of her work-free weekend.

"Dear Sir," Sally Ann wrote as she drafted a phony fax to send to Dan Geist announcing that she and not Luke would be in New Orleans to receive the arbitration results. "I wish to say that, although you are a consummate horse's ass, you appear to be a decent attorney; this is fortunate for you since you would have been disbarred were your professional skills on par with your personal gracelessness."

She quickly tore up her note and tossed the pieces into the trash can. She turned on her computer, then began to type: "Dear Mr. Geist: Please be advised that I rather than Luke Johnson will represent this company at the arbitration panel's final meeting in New Orleans next week . . ." She finished the note, saved it, then entered the fax instructions into her computer.

Sally Ann looked at her watch. Two hours and 50 minutes until quitting time. She sighed, picked up a file, and went back to work.

Chapter Four

Jimmy Buffett Nights

Not the Parrot Head Mecca

"Jimmy Buffett has opened a Margaritaville Café in New Orleans," Sally Ann said to Joe after the flight attendant had served them their Cokes and airline peanuts.

"And how did you find out this nugget of information—from reading that Jimmy Buffett newsletter you subscribe to?" Joe asked. "What's it called, 'The Mango Monologue?'"

"Very funny," Sally Ann said. "It's 'The Coconut Telegraph.' I found out about the Café from the liner notes on the 'Fruitcakes' CD. And I don't subscribe to 'The Coconut Telegraph.' I just got a free copy of it so I could find out Jimmy's summer touring schedule."

"I suppose we'll have to visit this Parrot Head Mecca while we're in New Orleans, then," Joe said, smiling fondly at his wife.

"Actually, for a Buffett fan, the New Orleans restaurant would be a third-tier shrine. I think the real Parrot Head Mecca would be the block on Duval Street in Key West, where Jimmy used to play at Howie's Lounge," Sally Ann said, looking seriously at her husband to hide that she was teasing him. "Second would be his first Margaritaville Café and store in Key West, which are also on Duval Street."

"I worry about you, Sally Ann. Am I going to turn on the news one night and see you getting hauled away by the police, claiming you're Mrs. Jimmy Buffett?"

"Since I'm already Mrs. Stanton, that's most unlikely. Although I wouldn't mind it if you'd sing me a few lines of some of his songs."

"I think that your job has sent you over the edge, Sally."

"No," she answered. "I'm teetering on the brink, but I haven't fallen off the cliff. Yet."

"Well, try to teeter until we find a way to get you out of there. In the meantime, let's enjoy our semi-free trip to New Orleans."

"Thanks for taking the time off from work to come with me, honey. I really appreciate it."

"I'd rather stroke you than my computer keys," Joe said, reaching out and squeezing his wife's thigh under cover of the tray table.

Sally Ann leaned over and whispered lewd suggestions in her husband's ear. Joe's face turned red but he smiled happily. "Later, babe, and that's guaranteed." Joe saw that his wife was starting to relax the farther away she got from her job. He tilted his seat back and closed his eyes, trying to settle his large, muscular frame in the economy class seat. "What do you think we'll get for dinner back here in steerage?"

Guilt is the Operative Emotion

"Sometimes I just feel like walking away from everything and everybody," Sally Ann said quietly. "Everybody except you and Bubba, of course.

"I'm so tired, Joe. I feel as if I've been in a vise for over 20 years and the screws just keep on tightening. Since I was fourteen, there hasn't been a year without grinding pressure, and I don't see an end to it."

"Your father made everything worse," Joe said, stroking his wife's hair as she lay pressed against him in bed in their New Orleans hotel room. "Things were bad for you at home. Then when we got married—two 20 year old kids trying to start a marriage and finish college—your dad roped you into caring for your mother when she had another breakdown six weeks after our wedding."

"My dad would never hospitalize my mother," Sally Ann said angrily, "even when she was raving and hallucinating. I'd tell my dad she needed to go to EPPI, and he'd just shrug and say, 'It never does her any good.'"

"I guess your father didn't care that it might have done his daughters some good," Joe said, his voice tight and angry.

"There were several times that first year we were married that my sister Olivia would call me, sobbing into the telephone that she couldn't take it and was going to run away. And I'd hear my mother howling in the background and my dad yelling at her to shut up while he hit her."

"I remember Livvie calling. But I didn't know he hit your mother. I'm so sorry."

"Oh, yeah. And then I'd hang up and call her doctor and say, 'Look, my mom's really sick this time, just completely not functioning. You've got to tell my dad that she has to be admitted to the hospital.' And the doctor would do it, and then you and I would take her to the psych ward since my father 'just couldn't deal with it,' and then there'd be some peace for four or six weeks until she came home."

"Your dad really shit on you, Sally."

"He shit on everybody, not just me. He specialized in biting the hand that fed him."

"Yeah, well, he dumped on you more than your sisters. You were the one who stayed in Philly after the others left. You were the one who visited several times a week, cooked the holiday meals, managed their finances after your dad got sick, spent every Sunday with them.

"There were a lot of times I wanted to tell your father to fuck off and to quit trying to ruin your life and our marriage. But I didn't want to interfere since your family was so important to you. I'm sorry now that I didn't."

"I'm sorry for all the time and energy I spent on my parents, Joe. I should never have taken so much away from us. But at the time I thought it was the right thing to do—I thought 'decent' people helped out their families.

"Do you know what my reward was, Joe?" Sally Ann added bitterly. "Once, several years after my dad got sick, we were looking at the family photo album. He pointed to a picture of himself, my mom and my two older sisters, taken before I was born, and said, 'That's when we really had a family.'"

"What did you say? I hope you told him that his 'true family' had left town because your sisters couldn't cope with his and your mother's problems."

"I didn't say anything. I couldn't talk."

"If it's any consolation to you, when I got my first job out of college, instead of congratulating me your father told me I didn't have what it takes to make it in a major engineering firm."

"That bastard. Why didn't you tell me? After all you'd done for my folks—hauling my mother to the hospital, shoveling their snow, running their errands. If I'd known I'd have reamed him royally. I wasn't very good at standing up for myself back then but I always tried to look out for you."

"I know," Joe said gently. "That's why I didn't tell you."

"And now I work for Luke, the latest in a succession of jerk bosses. You know, I really thought that after my dad died and the doctors found a medication that could control my mother's depressions, I'd finally get a little bit of peace. What an ass I was.'

"Don't call yourself names," Joe said sharply. "I won't tolerate it." He sat up and turned on the bedside lamp, picking up a newsmagazine he'd been reading and handing it to Sally Ann. "I was going to show you this later but now might be a good time.

"There's an article in this magazine about how many lawyers are leaving your profession each year and how unhappy most of the ones who stay are. But you already know that. The reason I wanted you to see this is because the article quotes a psychologist who does job counseling for unhappy attorneys. He was a lawyer himself and hated it, so he went back to grad school and got a Ph.D. There are so many depressed attorneys that he can make a living by limiting his practice to lawyers."

"A shrink whose patients are burned-out attorneys. That sounds like a joke, or a sketch from an old 'Saturday Night Live,'" Sally Ann said. "Remember that article you brought me from the San Francisco newspaper after your last business trip to California? The one that quoted a Marin County dominatrix who said the majority of her clients were lawyers and psychologists? I guess with this guy she'd have to give a two-for-one discount."

"Very funny, Sally Ann. The reason I want you to read this is because this psychologist has his office in Philadelphia. I think you should consider going to see him."

"Well thanks a lot," Sally Ann said indignantly. "You think I'm some whining yuppie who needs to go to a shrink and grouse for years about the trauma of having to choose between a BMW and a Volvo?"

"Oh calm down, Sally," Joe said with irritation in his voice. "According to the article, this man doesn't do personal therapy. He does job counseling, to get lawyers to see if there are any other non-law jobs that would suit them. Considering how much you hate Luke and since you haven't been able to find another legal job, I think it would be worth your while to go see this man. At least you could gripe to him and not me about your boss."

"Well excuse me. I won't bother you anymore with my petty troubles."

"Oh for Chrissakes, Sally, that's not what I mean. I just get tired of hearing how unhappy you are when there's nothing I can do to help. Maybe this man will have some ideas on how you can make your life better."

Joe leaned over and looked at his wife's tense face. "I feel like I really dropped the ball by not protecting you from your family. I don't want that to happen again."

"You didn't drop the ball, Joe," she said, reaching over to touch his face. "You know I'm so stubborn I would have gotten my back up if you'd tried to keep me from helping out my folks."

"You are stubborn, that's for damn sure. When you dig your heels in even a neutron bomb couldn't knock you off balance. But I think both your parents really manipulated you."

"Yeah, they did," Sally Ann said. "And I knew they were doing it. But I just felt so bad about all their problems the guilt almost killed me every time I tried to back off."

"What is it with you Catholics and guilt, Sally?"

"Guilt is the operative emotion in the Catholic church," Sally Ann said sourly, rolling over onto her back. "And even though I thought the church was totally off base from the time I was really little, sixteen years in Catholic schools took their toll. You know the saying, 'You can take the Catholic out of the church, but you can't take the guilt out of the Catholic.'"

"That's just foreign to me, babe," Joe said.

"Of course it is. You went to public schools with normal teachers, and on Sundays you went to Sunday schools where the kids sang

'Jesus Loves Me' and there were pictures of ducks and bunnies on the walls.

"I, on the other hand, was taught by emotionally-disturbed nuns who interjected sin and guilt into every lesson. Every day I stared at the bloody crucifixes and pictures of slaughtered saints on the walls, plus the whole school had to go to mass every school day and on Sundays too. And the nuns slapped us around. I was convinced I was damned by the time I was eight."

She added, "Most of the Jesuits were too intelligent to get off on the blood and guilt crap. So even though you went to a Catholic college, you didn't get the real parochial school experience that all of us recovering Catholics had."

"What about the anti-abortion propaganda, and all the pictures of bloody fetuses plastered all over the theology and biology departments in college?"

"That was gross, but it was still Catholic school lite. For the real experience, you'd have to have been burned on the altar of Sister Mary Moloch along with the other first-graders."

"I've never understood why your parents sent their girls to such awful schools."

"Because the church said Catholic children had to be educated in Catholic schools, and my father always did everything the church said. He spent his whole life trying to atone for his perceived failure of not making it through the seminary. Since he wasn't a priest, and was thus a second-class person who'd let down God, he over-compensated by being super Catholic.

"Besides, he felt guilty about having children. We were living proof that he'd had sex, and so had failed to achieve his goal of being either a Jesuit or an early Christian martyr."

"I thought having sex, particularly with children, was almost a prerequisite for being a Catholic priest," Joe said drily.

"Illicit pedophile sex has always been ignored by the church authorities. But God forbid a priest, or a clerical wannabe, should have a loving marriage and a happy family life."

"That is so sick, baby," Joe said, nuzzling Sally Ann's neck. "Loving you is the most intelligent thing I've done in my life. I wouldn't be half the man I am if we hadn't gotten together."

Sally Ann fought back the impulse to say something flippant, always her first inclination when deep emotions were at issue. She pressed herself against her husband, feeling the warmth of his solid male body. He slid his hands under her camisole, fondling her breasts as he kissed her face and neck. Sally Ann felt his erection against her thigh.

"I think I'm going to collect on that promise you made on the plane," Joe gasped as he pulled off her bikini pants. He rolled on top of her; Sally Ann opened her legs and wrapped them around her husband. She grabbed his buttocks as he pushed into her, pulling him deeper into her heat. She climaxed almost immediately. Joe lost control, his erection getting even harder as he thrust fiercely into his wife. Sally Ann moaned continually, her hips rising to accept her husband's body.

"Oh, God," Joe groaned as Sally Ann and he climaxed together. He lay on top of her, his face pressed into her neck as he gasped for breath. Sally Ann kept her arms wrapped around Joe's muscular back; she hugged him fiercely, thinking how much she loved him.

"My life would be so empty without you," Sally Ann whispered. Joe muttered sleepily and rolled off her. Within seconds he was snoring. Sally Ann smiled and nestled her face into his thick chest hair. She fell asleep, curled next to her husband's comforting warmth.

Miss Piggy's Guide to Life

"How do I look?" Sally Ann stood in front of Joe who laid down the New Orleans Times-Picayune and eyed his wife.

"Good enough to eat," he said, giving her an exaggerated leer.

"That can be arranged," she said as she leaned over to kiss the top of his head. "After I get back from my meeting, a repeat of last night would be wonderful.

"But for now, how do I look?" she asked again.

"Great," Joe said. "Very neat, very pretty, very professional."

"Flattery will get you everywhere," Sally Ann said with a laugh. She picked up her purse and briefcase, saying, "I've got to go. My meeting's in 45 minutes."

Joe stood up. "I'll walk you out and call you a cab."

"You don't need to, sweetie," Sally Ann said. "Stay here and be comfortable."

"I know I don't need to, but I want to. As good as you look, some Big Sleazy masher might put the moves on you in the lobby."

"Oh, big strong man protecting his little woman?" Sally Ann asked teasingly.

"I know you can take care of yourself. I'll just be along to give the guy-stare to any man who looks at you."

"The guy-stare? What's that?"

"It's where one male glares fiercely at another male who's eyeing his woman."

"Followed by . . . what? Butting chests? Clashing antlers?"

"When needed." Joe thrust his chest and jaw out, bristling his thick mustache.

Sally Ann laughed, "Let's go, then, moose."

After the doorman motioned in a cab, Joe tipped him. He walked Sally Ann to the curb, and held the cab door for her. She kissed him on the cheek, then brushed his face, saying "lipstick." Both of them were already sweating in the thick, steamy New Orleans heat.

"I expect to be finished by noon," Sally Ann said. "How about lunch at Galatoire's?"

"Sounds good to me. Why don't you take a cab from your meeting and meet me at the restaurant?" Joe closed the cab door and waved to his wife as the vehicle pulled into traffic.

Sally Ann gave the address to the driver, a middle-aged white man who spoke with the honking, nasal accent of New Orleans' Irish Channel. He sounded as if he came from Brooklyn rather than Louisiana. "First time in N'Awleans?" he asked, giving the city's name a southern as well as Brooklyn intonation.

"No, I've been here before on business. But this time my husband and I will get to spend several vacation days here."

"Well, I tell all my passengers, don't drink the tap water."

"Really? Is the city sewage system bad?"

"It's Mississippi River water, chere. Think of how many kidneys that water has passed through on its trip from the North to the South."

"I never thought of it that way," Sally Ann said, feeling slightly queasy. "I guess I'll start brushing my teeth with bottled water."

"Might be a good idea."

The driver piloted his cab carefully and skillfully through the already-hot New Orleans streets. It was mid-morning; there weren't many people out in the business district, either on the streets or sidewalks. Sally Ann assumed most of them were ensconced in their air-conditioned offices. The few pedestrians strolled slowly; Sally Ann wondered how their lungs could take in enough oxygen from the almost liquid air that had smacked her in the face like a wet sponge as she left the hotel. "How do you cope with this heat?" she asked.

"This isn't bad," the driver answered cheerfully. "You want heat, come here in August."

"How did people cope before air-conditioning?"

"The Uptown folks generally left town for the summer. The rest of us sweat buckets and moved as little as possible during the afternoons."

"I hate heat and humidity," Sally Ann said. "I think I would have turned into an axe murderer."

"A lot of us would have," the driver said, honking a nasal laugh, "except that it would've taken too damn much energy."

They reached the sterile glass office tower that was Sally Ann's destination. She paid and tipped the driver. As he was writing her receipt, he said, "I heard you and your husband talking about lunch at Galatoire's. You two be careful down in the Quarter. There's a lot of street crime down there, especially at night. The Chamber of Commerce tries to keep it hushed up so the tourists won't get scared off."

"You mean it's dangerous even at noon?" Sally Ann asked.

"With your husband you should be all right. If I was a lady I wouldn't go around too much on my own. After dark both of you should be real careful."

"Déjà vu," Sally Ann said. "It sounds like Philadelphia, where I'm from." She added, "I thought all the good restaurants are in the French Quarter."

"Not all of them. Christian's in Metairie, across Lake Pontchartrain, is good. It used to be an old church, now it's a restaurant. You and your husband can get there by taking a cab from your hotel."

"The food's good?" Sally Ann asked.

"This is N'Awleans, chere, where everyone's a restaurant critic. If the food's bad, a place won't stay in business."

"Well, thanks for the information." Sally Ann got out of the cab and walked quickly into the building's air-conditioned lobby, gratefully sucking the cool, dehumidified air into her lungs.

When she opened the heavy wood doors to the fifteenth-floor law firm where Geist and she were meeting the arbitrators, Sally Ann stopped in surprise for a few seconds. She was stepping from the bland corridor of a building that could have been in any suburban office park anywhere in the U. S. into what looked like the drawing room of an antebellum mansion.

The firm's two-story reception area had dully-polished wide-plank wood floors that were partly covered with worn Oriental rugs in muted jewel tones. A round mahogany table sat in the middle of the otherwise empty floor. Leather wing chairs were placed against the white-plastered, dark-woodworked walls. A winding wooden stairway connected the first floor to the wrought-iron railinged second-level gallery overlooking the receptionist's highly-lustered cherry and walnut counter.

Sally Ann gave her name to the young blonde woman sitting behind the curving reception station. "I'll have you escorted to the conference room right away, Miss Stanton," the young woman said.

"Mrs.," Sally Ann replied with a smile.

"Oh," the receptionist said. "I'm so sorry. Most of our lady lawyers aren't married." She pressed a button and spoke quietly into her mouthpiece.

What about the ones who aren't ladies? Sally Ann thought. Do the sluts have husbands? She smiled again but said nothing.

"Will you follow me, please, Miss Stanton," a second flashy young blonde asked.

"Mrs.," Sally Ann said. "It's Mrs. Stanton."

"Oh, I'm sorry," the young woman said. "Most of our ladies aren't married."

This is going to get old very fast, Sally Ann thought.

She followed the young woman up the stairs, amazed that the girl could move in her tight, short skirt and stiletto heels. Like the receptionist, this young woman had big hair, long polished fingernails, and wore heavy, bright makeup. Sally Ann felt like a librarian at a Hooters' convention with her tailored tan suit, medium-heeled pumps and short dark hair. She raised her free hand and briefly touched her pearl necklace, as always reassured by its weight and drape against her ivory silk blouse.

Sally Ann's guide led her to a door at the far end of the gallery, which provided an external corridor for the offices and work areas opening from it. Sally Ann caught glimpses of the usual silk-stocking law firm routine: harried-looking young men in starched shirtsleeves and braces dumping files on their assistants' overflowing desks, well-dressed senior secretaries bustling importantly as they carried out the partners' directions. This being the South, people appeared to be more soft-spoken than was the rule in other parts of the country, but the courtesy was a veneer overlying the standard law firm need to bill, bill, bill more hours to the over-charged clients who kept the business going.

"Here we are," the young blonde said, stopped before a closed wooden door. "If I may say so, your pearls are lovely."

"Thank you," Sally Ann replied. "They were a gift from my husband. It's always a special day when I can wear them."

"Ah, husbands," the blonde said in her soft New Orleans drawl. "They do have their uses."

"'The only thing better than being with the one you love is using his credit cards,'" Sally Ann said with a smile.

"Who said that?" the young woman asked, tapping her gold and diamond necklace with a long red nail as she smiled knowingly.

"Miss Piggy." The two women laughed and the blonde began her swaying return to the stairs. Sally Ann knocked on the door, then entered.

Dan Geist and his flunky, a young lawyer named Pete McBride whom Geist seldom allowed to speak, were already seated at the mahogany conference table.

"Mr. Geist, Mr. McBride," Sally Ann said as she entered the room. "Good morning."

The two men stood briefly. "Good morning, Mrs. Stanton."

"Where are the arbitrators?" Sally Ann asked.

"They've been delayed. But they should be here in about 20 minutes," Geist answered. "It's no big deal. I doubt if our meeting will last ten minutes once they're finally here."

So what was the point of our traipsing down to New Orleans? Sally Ann thought, although she already knew the answer. The point, on Geist's part, was to run up the billable hours charged to his client. Had Luke Johnson attended the meeting, the point would have been to get him a company-paid trip to an interesting city and to increase his sense of self-importance as he traveled first class on someone else's money. Oh, well, Sally Ann thought, now Joe and I are getting a semi-free trip and I'm out of the office until Monday. If the company and Geist's client are willing to pay, I'll take advantage of the opportunity.

"How was your flight from Chicago?" she asked the two men politely. "Did you come in last night or early this morning?"

"Last night." Geist, as always, answered. "I didn't feel like getting up at 5:00 a.m. to catch the first morning flight."

The three lawyers sat at the long polished conference table, making conversastion as they waited for the arbitrators' arrival. Geist alternately tried to bully and condescend to Sally Ann. She found that she could gauge his view of his attempted domination by his treatment of the silent McBride. If Sally Ann scored a verbal point, Geist would snap something insulting to his associate. When she was unable to rebut one of Geist's sallies, he would address a complimentary remark to McBride.

You must really want that partnership, McBride, Sally Ann thought as Geist finished telling a demeaning anecdote about how his twelve-year old daughter had insulted Pete at her birthday party the previous month.

There was a knock at the door, but the person entering was the court reporter rather than the arbitrators. The man, who was graying and a little paunchy, introduced himself and collected the lawyers' business cards after setting up his transcribing equipment.

"How y'all doin' this mawnin'?" the reporter asked. "Had a chance to enjoy any of our good N'Awleans restaurants?"

Geist immediately and pompously began telling the court reporter about McBride's and his dinner the night before at Antoine's. He lovingly detailed the expensive wines they drank, recited the appetizers and entrees each ordered, lingered over his description of dessert and café brulot, followed by cognac and cigars. You would be the type to smoke cigars, Sally Ann thought, since she had a theory that the men who smoked large, phallic-shaped cigars were symbolically exposing their own sexual organs to a presumably-admiring world, although in her opinion they always looked as if they were fellating another man as they sucked on their tobacco cylinders.

Sally Ann rescued the reporter, whose eyes were slightly glazing as Geist's monologue ended. "Does most of your work involve the kind of commercial arbitration we're doing today?" she asked.

"Recently, yes," the man answered. "N'Awleans got hid hard by the last recession and the downturn in the oil and gas industry during the '80s and early '90s. An awful lot of folks are trying to renegotiate their contracts.

"Until a few years ago I worked full time for one of the judges over at the courthouse. I recorded every proceeding he presided over. That was real interestin'—we did a lot of criminal work, some civil stuff. It was a lot more diverse than this contract business.

"But my daughter's in law school and I'm footin' her tuition bill, so I had to get a job that paid more. That's why I'm workin' for this agency now."

"What kind of law does your daughter hope to practice?" Sally Ann asked.

"She's not sure yet. I tell her to find a job where she can get out and see some people, not be stuck in an office all day with no company but a pile of papers. I spent all of yesterday at a deposition held in a windowless conference room where half the time the witness was just identifying files. I tell my girl to avoid that kind of job like the plague."

"How did your daughter get interested in doing legal work?" Sally Ann asked, mainly to forestall another of Geist's speeches.

"Damned if I know. She tended bar for several years after college. She's a pretty, fun-loving girl who likes to have a good time. I told her I thought she'd have a better time tending bar but that if law school was what she really wanted, I'd pay for it."

Sally Ann could tell from the indignant look on Geist's face that he was about to say something cutting to the reporter for daring to suggest his child could have a better life serving drinks than being an attorney. Geist lost his opportunity to speak when the conference room's door opened and the three arbitrators walked in.

"I apologize for our late arrival," the senior panel member said as he and the other two men shook hands with the lawyers and gave their cards to the court reporter. Sally Ann had recently read a newspaper article in which a woman professor of linguistics had opined that apologizing for lateness or other lapses was a form of servile female behavior to be avoided by correct businesswomen. She imagined the dignified arbitrator's disdain if someone told him his acceptance of responsibility for the panel's tardiness was not only slavish but also effeminate, rather than representing the courtesy that members of his generation had been taught to extend to all.

"Shall we begin?" the senior arbitrator asked. "After some deliberation, Mr. Guilfoyle, representing Ms. Stanton's company, Mr. Jameson, representing Mr. Geist's client, and I as the neutral arbitrator, have reached our decision.

"We find that, in light of the adverse conditions in petitioner's industry resulting from recent regulatory restrictions and import controls, the petitioner's claim of unforeseeable circumstances is well-founded. For this reason, it is the panel's decision that the contract in question shall be modified as follows: . . ." The arbitrator then read a list of contractual changes giving Sally Ann's company around 60 percent of the relief it had sought.

"However, we also find that these adverse circumstances are not severe enough to justify granting petitioner all the relief it has requested. For this reason, the following sections of the disputed contract shall remain unchanged: . . . ." Geist's client would thus continue to receive about 40 percent of the benefit of its original agreement. "Assuming neither party moves for reconsideration, Ms. Stanton and Mr. Geist, you should both get copies of the transcript and of this panel's final order within the next ten days."

As Luke had predicted, both sides got something in the arbitrators' compromise decision, although he had previously told Sally Ann that he didn't expect to get more than half of what their company's petition requested. Sally Ann could tell that Geist was annoyed at the 60-40 split but doubted that he would protest the decision, since arbitration rulings were seldom modified by a panel and there were few grounds for appealing to a court for review.

"Thank you, gentlemen and Mrs. Stanton," Geist said as he stood. "I'll notify my client of your decision." He shook hands with each of the arbitrators and Sally Ann, then left the room, leaving the mute McBride to pick up the files.

"Thank you, gentlemen," Sally Ann said, shaking hands with each of the panel members. All of them gave Sally Ann slightly avuncular, slightly lecherous looks as each held her small hand a little longer than customary for a business handshake. She didn't take offense, having learned early on that her combination of intelligent good looks and brains either reduced men to stuttering idiots or intimidated them into trying to dominate her. Since being stared at was less tiring than standing up to the bullies she preferred the admiration. Sally Ann sometimes wondered what kind of swath she could have cut through the male sex if she hadn't married young and been constrained by the scruples of her strict Catholic upbringing.

"Goodbye, Pete," she said to McBride. "Have a safe trip back to Chicago. And make Geist carry his own luggage." McBride smiled sheepishly, then held the door for Sally Ann as she left the conference room.

She made her way back across the gallery and down the stairs to the reception desk. "I need to send a fax to my office. Could you transmit this for me?" Sally Ann handed the receptionist a brief note asking Claudia to notify Luke in Seattle of the favorable arbitration ruling.

The blonde receptionist reached out her manicured hand, her heavy gold bracelets clanking, and took the sheet of paper.

"Do those nails get in your way?" Sally Ann looked at the blonde's pink-lacquered talons.

"Not really," the young woman said languidly. "I never do anything heavy with my hands—that's what my boyfriend is for."

"Ah," Sally Ann said, mentally picturing a beefy young man toiling in the hot Louisiana sun while the blonde drank iced tea on a shaded veranda and pulled the invisible silken strings binding him to her.

"Your fax has been sent and received," the receptionist said.

"Thanks so much. Could you call a cab for me? I need to meet my husband at Galatoire's for lunch."

"I hope your husband is already there, or y'all will have a long wait outside."

"Why's that?"

"Galatoire's doesn't take reservations for lunch. There's usually a line of people waiting to get in from about noon on."

"Oh, dear. Well, I guess we'll have to take our chances."

"The food is worth the wait."

"Is that a promise?"

"Absolutely. This is N'Awleans, after all."

When Sally Ann got out of the cab in the steaming French Quarter, as the receptionist had predicted, there was a long line of hungry people stretching from Galatoire's front door down the sidewalk. She scanned the crowd, looking for Joe.

A tall man wearing a leather-billed khaki ballcap waved. It was Joe, standing in line about half-way to the restaurant's entrance.

"What's with the hat?" Sally Ann asked, noticing that it had 'Air Margaritaville' embroidered on the front.

"I got tired of sitting around the hotel so I took a cab to the Jimmy Buffett store. I bought my hat and this one for you." Joe handed her a tropical print ballcap with 'The Parrot Head Club' embroidered on the bill. "Here. Put it on."

"You're wearing khakis and a golf shirt. I have on a business suit and pearls. I don't think the hat exactly complements my outfit."

"Oh, I don't know about that. I think it expresses your true nature." Joe smiled and nudged his wife gently in the ribs. "Besides, look at these people. You'll still look pretty conservative compared to most of them."

Sally Ann looked up and down the line. There were businessmen in tropical suits, old matrons with heavy makeup and huge hats sitting on their blue hair, sloppily-dressed tourists in garish T-shirts, overdressed ladies who lunch, two people she thought were drag queens, and several elderly men, probably gay, who projected an air of ruined elegance. The line had moved enough that Sally Ann could see into Galatoire's, with its white linen-covered tables crammed closely on the tiled floors under the rotating ceiling fans, the talking, laughing patrons reflected in the mirrored walls as they ate, smoked and gestured with abandon. Sally Ann thought that Toulouse-Lautrec would have appreciated Galatoire's—she half expected to see an early-rising Jane Avril dancing around the tables, dodging the white-jacketed waiters.

"You're right," she said to Joe. "No one will notice me." She put on her Parrot Head cap. "So tell me about the store."

"Well," Joe said, "since I'm only an incipient Buffett fan and not a full-fledged Parrot Head, I might have missed the full significance of the experience. But," he added teasingly, "there was a young blonde in a tight T-shirt who asked me if I'd like to get Buffetted."

"And what did you say?" Sally Ann asked with a mock glare.

"I said thank you very much, miss, but I only Buffett with my wife."

"Did that cool her down?" Sally Ann said.

"Not really. She started singing 'Why Don't We Get Drunk and Screw' right there in the store."

"And . . . ?"

"And I said, 'Why, miss, you're attractive enough I'd do you sober if I weren't married.' That seemed to piss her off and she left in a huff."

Sally Ann put her arm around her husband's waist. "You know, if you didn't have those big brown eyes and all those muscles, flashy young women wouldn't always be making eyes at you."

"They can look all they want," Joe said, stroking the back of his wife's sleek dark head. "I like brunettes."

"Oh, so you didn't notice this girl's assets?"

"Do you mean did I see that she wasn't wearing a bra? I'm only human."

"Pig," Sally Ann said, giving Joe a gentle punch in the ribs.

"Piggette," Joe retaliated. "A woman who goes to soccer games hoping the players will sweat through their uniforms shouldn't be calling me names."

"It was only once. Besides, one team was wearing white nylon shorts. I'd have to have been blind not to notice their uniforms turned see-through when they started sweating."

"What were you doing looking at their butts?"

"I'm only human."

Sally Ann and Joe smiled at each other. "Well, human, we're almost to the front of the line," Joe said. "Let's eat our Creole lunch and talk about what to do for the rest of our weekend in New Orleans."

"As long as I don't have to talk or think about work, I don't care. We can sit in the hotel room and stare at the walls and I'll enjoy it."

"I think we can do better than that," Joe said quietly as the maitre d' led them to their table.

Sally Ann looked at the varied eccentrics dining at Galatoire's, all of them apparently losing their private troubles in the pleasure of a good meal and pleasant company. "You're right. We will do better than that." She scanned the menu an elderly black waiter had handed her, then looked around the dining room again. "Everyone in this room and this city seems to follow Miss Piggy's motto: 'More is more.'"

Joe raised his water glass to his wife. "To excess."

"To excess," Sally Ann replied. "Let's enjoy it while we can."

Chapter Five

Out of Sync, Out of Place, Out of Answers

I'm Dysfunctional, Who Isn't?

"*My* approach to job counseling is this: I have my clients take standardized psychological tests and then assess their career possibilities in light of their personality traits. Generally, people will never be satisfied unless the requirements of their jobs mesh with their values and personalities. This may sound obvious but it isn't to a lot of my clients, many of whom have chosen careers for which they're completely unsuited.

"Now, before you tell me about yourself I'll give you a little bit of my background so you'll have an idea of what you're getting into."

Sally Ann looked at the slight dark-haired man sitting across the desk from her. "Sounds good to me," she said, trying to mask her uneasiness at being in a place where she might actually have to talk about her feelings. She looked at his embossed name plate reading 'Mark Green, J.D., Ph.D.' "So you're a lawyer as well as a psychologist," she said, just to make conversation, since she had known since her New Orleans trip that he had once practiced law.

"Absolutely," Dr. Green answered. "And for now I only counsel attorneys who want to change their specializations within the law or get into completely new lines of non-legal work."

"There are enough unhappy lawyers that you can make a living limiting your practice like that?"

"Absolutely." Dr. Green repeated one of his favorite words. "National statistics show that every year as many attorneys leave the profession as new lawyers are licensed to practice law. And informal surveys taken by various state bar associations suggest that from 50 to 70 percent of the attorneys who continue as lawyers are unhappy with their work and would leave it if they could find another way to support themselves."

"And I thought I was the only one," Sally Ann said, beginning to feel that Joe hadn't been a complete bully when he kept pressing her to call Dr. Green after they got back from New Orleans.

"You have lots of company.

"So, to get back to my background," Green continued, "I am a fourth-generation lawyer. My family expected me to go to law school and join the family firm, so I did.

"I disliked law school but told myself things would be better when I was an actual attorney. I didn't like practicing law but kept thinking things would get better eventually. After ten years, when I'd built up a successful trial practice and been a partner in the firm for several years, I finally admitted to myself that I didn't like being a lawyer and wanted to work as a psychologist, which was my major in college.

"I quit my job, enrolled in grad school, and got my Ph.D. Then one night while I was lying in bed trying to decide how to market my new business, it hit me: I'd combine my two fields and only work with lawyers. And so far I've had as much business as I can handle."

Sally Ann looked away, realizing she had been staring fixedly at Green's face. She was used to being the person who did the talking and asked the questions, and disliked being in the subordinate position.

Dr. Green continued. "Now, tell me about yourself. I don't do personal counseling but I feel that I need to have at least some idea of who my clients are, and also of who they think they are, if I'm to be of any help to them.

"So, are you from a legal family?"

"Yes," Sally Ann said. "My father was a lawyer."

"And were you expected to follow in his footsteps?"

"I don't think so. My dad had a rather low opinion of women in general, and he particularly didn't like the idea of women lawyers."

"Was your father a successful lawyer?"

"Professionally he was quite well-regarded. But financially he never did well since he turned down every opportunity he ever had to make money, including leaving several lucrative partnerships."

"Why do you think he did that?" Green asked with more than professional interest in his voice.

"He had religious hang-ups about financial success, you know, the 'camel through the eye of the needle' crap. Plus, he had wanted to be a Catholic priest but was asked to leave the seminary because the administrators felt he wasn't suited to the life. I think he spent the rest of his life unconsciously punishing himself for his 'failure.' One of the ways he did so was by trashing his career." Sally Ann added in embarrassment, "That sounds like the script from a particularly bad soap opera, but it's all true."

"Soap opera writers couldn't come up with anything as ludicrous as real life," Green said.

"Then, on top of his religious scruples," Sally Ann said, "when he was in his mid-30s my dad decided he was a socialist, even though he'd grown up in a big house in Villanova and hung with a crowd of rich Catholic preppies when he was young."

Green guffawed, then said apologetically, "I'm really sorry."

"Don't apologize," Sally Ann said. "I told you my family history is ludicrous. My father went from being a country club Republican to being the only socialist on the Tax Committee of the Philadelphia Bar Association."

"Your father was a tax lawyer?"

"Yes. He had religious and political scruples against making money, but spent his professional life advising the wealthy on how to lower their tax liabilities."

Green laughed again, then said, "Oh, dear, I'm not usually this unprofessional."

"My dad was probably the only lawyer in this city who routinely got the Pennsylvania Bar Association's newsletters and also subscribed to the Manchester Guardian," Sally Ann said, referring to a socialist newspaper published in Britain. "This was during the J. Edgar Hoover years so I'm sure that buried in the FBI archives there's a file on my father—his copies of the Guardian were always a month late and had clearly been read before they got delivered to our house."

"So what made you decide to go to law school?" Dr. Green asked Sally Ann.

"I'm not sure. I guess I first got the idea as a child—I was very argumentative and my mother was always telling me I'd grow up to be a lawyer like my father.

"Then as I got older my dad was always after me and my sisters to get a skill so we could support ourselves. He kept telling us that we had to be independent and able to take care of ourselves because he wasn't going to once we grew up."

Dr. Green said musingly, "So, you and your sisters were 'only women' on the one hand, but on the other you were expected to be independent and self-sufficient. It sounds as if your father gave you a lot of mixed messages."

"That was my dad—king of the mixed messages."

She added, "My childhood was one long mixed message. My dad was always harping that there was no money and that he was making enormous sacrifices to send us to Catholic schools—except that he'd only let us go to our crummy parish school, not to any of the good Catholic academies—and to support us in general. He made my sisters and me feel like greedy parasites for needing food and clothing. It wasn't until I grew up that I found that the low income was voluntary on his part.

"It was all kind of schizophrenic: we had piano lessons on the one hand but on the other my dad wouldn't give my mother enough money for food. We never went hungry but we ate a lot of cornbread and beans."

"And was your father pleased despite himself when you graduated from law school? I see from your resume that you were on the dean's list and in the top fourth of your class. That must have made him happy."

"If it did, he never told me so," Sally Ann said quietly. "Even though I was married and also working part-time while I was in school, he was most concerned that I still be on call 24 hours a day to help out with my mother, who kept having very severe, recurring depressions. Then he had a heart attack and his general health started declining, and I got roped into helping out with that as well."

"It sounds like an enormous burden," Green said gently. "Did things get better once you got out of law school?"

"No. My mother's mental health got even worse as my dad's physical health declined and I had to take on more and more responsibility for my parents, since by that time I was the only one of their children who hadn't left town. Plus I had several jobs where I did well professionally but I was working for lawyers who were very cold and controlling so the jobs were very stressful."

"Your bosses had personalities similar to your father's?"

"Yes, I guess so. I'd never thought of it that way." Sally Ann was surprised that something so obvious had never occurred to her. "Then my dad died, which was terribly painful, of course, and I got my present job. Unfortunately, my current boss is the worst person I've worked for. He's very erratic emotionally and can be quite abusive. Plus he hogs all of the good files for himself and refuses to delegate any real authority, so professionally I'm really frustrated."

Sally Ann sat quietly for a few seconds, then said slowly, "Basically, I'm just exhausted. I try to keep a good attitude but I don't know how much longer I can go on."

"Have you considered getting some personal therapy?" Dr. Green asked. "It sounds to me as if you've had an enormous amount of unrelieved stress in your life. Frankly, I'm surprised that you've managed to cope as well as you have."

"Oh, God," Sally Ann said, "the last thing I want is to be one of those whining yuppies who spend years in counseling."

"It seems to me," Green said gently, "that there's a difference between whining and admitting that you have current issues to deal with as a result of past events."

"Yeah, maybe," Sally Ann said dubiously. "But for now I think that I can only deal with the job counseling." She didn't add that once, in the early years of her marriage, she had mentioned to her sister Mariclaire that the family doctor had recommended that she take anti-depressants or see a therapist since she was so overwhelmed by her parents' problems. Mariclaire, who by that time was living 3,000 miles away in Oregon, had snickered and said nastily, "Well, I guess I'm the only strong one in the family."

"Well, if you change your mind I'd be happy to refer you to someone. In the meantime, to get started on my services, I'd like you to spend the rest of this session taking two standardized psychological tests: the Myers-Briggs, which establishes your general personality type, and the Graves, which gives additional insight into your psychological profile."

Oh great, Sally Ann thought, I'll probably get rated as completely dysfunctional since this guy thinks I need to see a shrink.

"Keep in mind," Green added, "there are no right or wrong answers on these tests."

That's what you say, Sally Ann thought, but I bet you've already got me tagged as a head case. She picked up the test booklets and answer sheets Dr. Green handed her, then followed him into a small conference room adjoining his office.

"You can sit at this table and take the tests. Here are several pencils for you to use when marking the answer sheets."

"The old number 2 pencils, I see," Sally Ann said. "I've spent half my life marking test sheets with number 2 pencils."

"Haven't we all." Dr. Green held out his hand for Sally Ann to shake. "I'm very pleased to have you as a client, and I look forward to working with you.

"When you finish the tests, please leave the forms with my secretary. I have another client coming in 20 minutes so I won't be able to see you before you leave. We'll go over the test results at your session next week."

Green left the room. Sally Ann sat down at the round conference table then glanced around the bookshelf-lined walls. There was no evidence of Dr. Green's former occupation; the shelves held only psychological journals and texts.

Sally Ann sank back into her cushioned chair and picked up the Myers-Briggs booklet. She read the instructions, then the first question. "People can usually tell what I am thinking. This statement is: (a) always true; (b) sometimes true; (c) seldom true; (d) never true." She marked (d), then went on to the second question.

"I get my energy from being around other people. This statement is: (a) always true; (b) sometimes true; (c) seldom true; (d) never true." Sally Ann marked (d) again. I hate this shit, she thought. She briefly considered not reading any more questions and instead marking the answer sheet so that the little penciled dots made a frowny-face, but then thought about how much Dr. Green was charging per hour. That's one lawyering lesson he hasn't forgotten. Oh, hell, I told Joe I'd give this my best shot so I will.

She worked through the Myers-Briggs test, then picked up the Graves booklet. More statements, but this time an answer sheet in the form of a graph. "I want to rely on my leader to look out for my best interests. This statement is (a) always true; (b) sometime true; (c) seldom true; (d) never true." Sally Ann marked (d).

"I prefer to achieve my goals through group meetings and the consensus of everyone involved. This statement is . . ." Sally Ann marked (d).

Halfway through the Graves test her mind started to wander. These questions are ridiculous, she thought. They're irrelevant to anything that's going on in my life. She started making up questions for the Sally Ann Psychological Profile.

"Complete this sentence. I'm dysfunctional, (a) you suck; (b) who isn't; (c) what's your point; (d) all of the above.

"My goal in life is to (a) be unemployed; (b) be well read; (c) relax; (d) all of the above.

"Before I die I want to: (a) go to another Jimmy Buffett concert; (b) get Jimmy Buffett's autograph; (c) meet Jimmy Buffett; (d) all of the above.

"My family is (a) humor-impaired; (b) humor-challenged; (c) humor-deficient; (d) all of the above.

"I will never forget: (a) the after-effects of my mother's shock treatments; (b) dragging my mother through the snow to the mental hospital one New Year's Day; (c) negotiating a real estate contract the morning after my mother attempted suicide; (d) all of the above."

Sally Ann's eyes filled with tears which she hastily blotted away with a Kleenex. Her thoughts had veered from the sardonic into the locked part of her mind where for years she had shoved all of the pain caused by her unfortunate family situation. It was a place that she seldom visited, although she dimly realized that her stored-up anguish was festering away under the surface of the tough mental skin she'd grown to conceal the sadness.

She went back to work on the Graves profile. When she finished the test, Sally Ann noticed that the markings on her answer graph were skewed, making a line that almost shot off the page. Jeez, what does that mean? Is my personality even more twisted than most lawyers'?

Picking up the papers, she left them with Dr. Green's assistant. "You look a little pale, Ms. Stanton," the woman said.

"I don't know why, but I found taking these tests really stressful," Sally Ann replied.

"Don't worry, most of Dr. Green's clients have the same reaction. You lawyers are all such control freaks you can't stand letting anyone else have access to your real personalities." The woman laughed.

"You're probably right," Sally Ann said weakly, unable to think of a witty comeback. "I'll see you next week."

Walking down the street, she looked at her watch—too late to go back to work. She went to the parking lot where she had left her car. Giving the attendant her ticket, she said, pointing, "It's that silver Acura Integra over there."

"Oh," the young man said. "So you're the lady who likes Jimmy Buffett."

Sally Ann remembered that she had left several Buffett tapes scattered on the passenger seat of her five-year old car. "Yes."

"He writes books now," the attendant said, eyeing the slim woman who stood in front of him, waiting for her car keys.

"I know," Sally Ann answered. "I've read them."

"I'm going to Key West some day."

"So am I," Sally Ann said as she handed over the parking fee plus tip. "It's a small place—you'll probably run into my husband and me." When he saw the extra money, the young man asked Sally if she wanted him to back her car out of its slot.

"No thanks. I'll get it." Sally Ann took her keys and walked over to her car. She waved to the attendant as she drove out of the open parking lot, then put Jimmy Buffett's 'Volcano' tape into her cassette player. She hummed along to 'Lady I Can't Explain,' wondering if getting insight into either her professional or personal life was worth the time and expense.

Buns 'n' Roses

"If only 'Top Gun' had been made five years later," Louise griped. "We might have been able to see some buns instead of all these damn towels." She hit the remote's fast-forward button; the film whizzed by until the movie's next scene of half-naked young men appeared. "Just look at all that firm young flesh," Louise murmured dreamily, her large grey eyes getting slightly glazed in the light of the candles she had flickering all over the room.

"How long has it been since you had a date?" Sally Ann asked her friend, who worked as an adjunct professor in the music studies department of one of the local colleges but whose real vocation was looking for a position that might lead to tenure at any college or university anywhere in the United States. The two of them were sitting in Louise's living room watching videos; Louise drank beer while Sally Ann sipped hot tea.

"Too long—I'm in a real love drought. I'm starting to think I'll never again get that wonderful post-sex feeling—you know, all warm and so relaxed I feel like I'm going to dissolve into the sheets."

"Yeah, I know," Sally Ann said, thinking longingly of Joe, who was on a business trip to Seattle. "What happened to your last boyfriend—that Swiss guy?"

"You mean Reinhard?"

"Yeah—the opera singer."

"He's currently porking a female cellist he met on his last tour," Louise answered grumpily.

"Oh, dear, I'm sorry," Sally Ann said.

"It's no big deal, really. We weren't exactly having the love affair of the year—or even of the month, for that matter. Reinhard was dumb as a fence post. All he could do was sing and fuck."

"Not at the same time, I hope."

Louise laughed. "No, he alternated. God, he had a beautiful voice."

"And a beautiful—?"

"That too. And he sure knew how to use it." Louise sighed, remembering pleasures past. "I wish he'd left it behind—it's the only part of him I miss."

"Someone else will turn up."

"I don't know. In my field most of the adult men I meet are gay, and I'm not about to start hitting on my students."

"Isn't 'adult men' an oxymoron—sort of like 'corporate culture' or 'legal ethics?'"

"You know what I mean—adult in years, not chronologically deficient, not age-impaired."

"You're into all that New Age stuff; why don't you start visualizing hot sex coming your way?" Sally Ann asked as she nestled deeper into Louise's overstuffed and sensually comfortable armchair.

"I tried that." Louise drained the last of her beer from the bottle.

"And . . . ?"

"All that happened is I ran into a flasher at the Free Library."

"Oh my God. What did you do?"

"I was just sitting at a table, reading the New York Times Sunday magazine, when I felt somebody staring at me. So I looked up, and this guy was sitting across the table from me. At first I didn't notice anything so he kind of glanced down at his lap—I looked down and then I saw this huge erection staring back at me."

"Jesus," Sally Ann said with disgust.

"You know what's really weird? At first I didn't believe what I was seeing. I actually thought I was hallucinating. So I got up and walked around the library for a few minutes.

"When I went back to my table, that bastard was actually still sitting there with his dick out. So then I got really mad. I walked right up to him and said, really loud, 'I just want you to know, I've seen better.'"

Sally Ann snickered. "Oh, Louise, that's great. What did he do?"

"Well, things deflated real fast, if you get my drift. He stuffed his equipment back into his pants and hightailed it out of the library."

"So did you talk to the librarian?"

"You bet I did. And all she said was, 'Oh my God, not another one. We just chased one of those perverts off two days ago.' And I was so furious. I said, 'Can't you call the cops and have them commit some police brutality on these creeps?'"

Louise twirled her empty beer bottle in her hands. "So that's what visualizing sex did for me."

"Well, I always said that New Age stuff is airy-fairy crap."

Louise and Sally Ann started laughing and then couldn't stop. They sat giggling helplessly, overcome by visions of deflating erections and straying operatic baritones.

"Oh, my God," Sally Ann gasped. "Look, we fast-forwarded all the way through 'Top Gun.'"

"That's okay. How about watching part of the 'Scarlett' miniseries. I taped it a while back when it was on TV."

"Is that the one with that English actor—one of the ex-James Bonds—as Rhett Butler?"

"You betcha," Louise said with lust in her voice. "Hunk city himself."

"Really? I never thought he had enough chest hair to play Rhett," Sally Ann said.

"Clark Gable didn't have any hair on his chest and he certainly made a great Rhett Butler."

"Yeah, he shaved it all off. What a waste. But a really authentic Rhett would've had thick chest hair—in *Gone With the Wind* Margaret Mitchell was always going on about the heavy dark hair on Rhett's muscular chest."

"Well, actually, so did Alexandra Ripley in *Scarlett*."

"Oh yeah? I never read it."

"It wasn't bad, but there wasn't enough sex in it. I mean, why do a modern sequel to a classic novel if you're not going to put any sex in it?"

"I totally agree."

Louise jumped to her feet. "I need another beer. Are you sure you don't want one?"

"No thanks. But I could use some more hot water and another tea bag," Sally Ann said, looking into the empty teapot sitting on a side table next to Louise's chair.

"Do you mind my asking why you don't drink, Sally Ann?" Louise asked.

"Partly it's to be contrary—since everyone I know drinks, I don't. But mainly it's because I don't have any tolerance for alcohol. I can take a few sips of wine and my eyes will start blurring and my hands shaking.

"Plus," Sally Ann added, "the few times I tried drinking it made me really depressed instead of happy or relaxed. To be perfectly frank, if I want to be sad I can go visit my relatives—I don't need a drink to do it."

Louise smiled sympathetically. "If it weren't for liquor, I couldn't cope when Daddy and his wife come to visit. I get a buzz on as soon as they walk in the door and I stay that way until they leave." She cuddled Othello, her small black poodle, as he sat in her lap. "Isn't that right, sweetie? Mommy feels no pain for days on end."

She picked up the remote control. "Well, if you don't want to watch 'Scarlett,' let's see what's on television." Louise started to scan the channels, stopping at an old movie that had a very young Sam Waterson and Jeff Bridges strolling through a western landscape. "What's this?" She leafed through her 'TV Guide,' then read, "'Rancho Deluxe'—an episodic tale of two amoral drifters in the modern West—three stars."

"I rented that several months ago, partly because my guide to old movies said it's a 'hip, comedic Western' and partly because the bar scene has Jimmy Buffett singing 'Livingston Saturday Night.' I wouldn't have given it three stars, though, probably two at most," Sally Ann said.

"Why's that?" Louise asked as she tried to figure out the movie's plot.

"It's a real '70s movie, and I wasn't particularly fond of the '70s . . . Come to think of it, I'm not sure I've ever been particularly fond of any decade.

"It seems like I'm always out of sync with the times. In the '70s everyone but me was getting loaded and screwing around. Then in the '80s, the decade of the ruthless, work-obsessed yuppie, Joe and I got married and I used up most of my energy helping out my folks. Now it's the '90s when all the aging boomers are supposedly rediscovering family values . . . but now I'm not interested in doing anything for anybody except myself and Joe. It seems like I'm always either five steps behind or two steps ahead of the prevailing mood."

"I know what you mean," Louise said, her Texas twang getting more pronounced as she drank her beer. "I don't even march to the beat of a different drummer—all I can hear is my own internal rhythm."

"That's why you're such a good pianist," Sally Ann said. "Neither one of us really fits in anywhere."

"Maybe we should start a support group for introverted female misfits with crazy families and dogs instead of children. You and I could be charter members."

Sally Ann laughed. "After we got our group together, we'd all sit in a circle facing outward. The first meeting would be a success if at least one person looked over her shoulder and said hello to another member."

"I'd probably get as much out of that as I have from all my years of therapy," Louise said.

"Speaking of which," Sally Ann said, "Joe prodded me into going to see a job counselor who only works with disgruntled lawyers. I had my first meeting with him last week."

"Is the sky falling?" Louise rolled her eyes toward the ceiling. "I never thought that was something you'd do."

"I never thought I'd do it either. I have to say I felt like shit after the first session even though the focus of the counseling is job-related and not personal. I had to listen to two Jimmy Buffett tapes to get back into a good mood after I left the man's office," Sally Ann said, not adding that she had relieved the rest of her tension that night in bed with Joe.

"What is it with you and Jimmy Buffett, Sally Ann?" Louise asked. "You and Elvis share the same birthday—why can't you obsess about the King like everybody else?"

"Maybe you and Joe should get together and try to analyze the situation," Sally Ann answered. "I was playing a Buffett CD a few night ago while I ran on my treadmill when Joe came stomping in— he asked if the stereo could be set a little lower than 'screech level' as he called it."

"When did you get a treadmill?" Louise asked. "I thought you swam several nights a week to stay in shape."

"I did until recently. But there were several old mashers who kept making passes at me; at first I thought it was funny but then they got really obnoxious. It's interesting—the younger guys were usually pretty respectful but the older ones were real jerks. And then the Y changed the chemicals it was putting in the pool and I started getting sneezing fits and horrible headaches every time I went swimming. So Joe and I bought the treadmill."

Sally Ann added, "I've given up on health clubs. I seem to be the kiss of death with regard to athletic facilities—each time I join one it either goes out of business or gets shut down by the health authorities. Now that the Y didn't work out either I'm going to exercise at home."

"I'm still going to my aerobics classes," Louise said. "I've worked through all the girls' levels—my current class is called 'Boot Camp' and has a lot of guys in it."

"Any cute ones?" Sally Ann asked.

"A few good butts and good shoulders. One or two have really good abs. But I don't think there are any dating possibilities there."

"You never know," Sally Ann said. "So," she added, "to change the subject, how does it feel to be a full-fledged Ph.D.?"

"Not Ph.D.—Ed.D.," Louise said. "And it feels damn good. I almost killed myself picking a thesis topic and getting it approved by my committee—that was actually harder than writing the damn book."

"Well, you didn't like the one I suggested," Sally Ann said.

"Yeah, right," Louise said derisively. "Something to do with Jimmy Buffett, as I recall."

"'From Bruckner to Buffett—A Twentieth Century Progression,'" Sally Ann recited. "I bet your thesis committee would have been impressed."

"Well, they'd never have forgotten it, I can tell you that much."

"And then you had to go and write about Liszt—traveling to Germany and England for your research when you could have gone to Florida and Texas."

"I grew up in Texas, remember?" Louise said with a laugh. "And I managed to escape. I'm never going back for anything but a visit." She sat quietly for a minute, idly running her fingers through Othello's soft black curls. "Speaking of visits, I've got a story for you."

"Tell me."

"The last time I went back home I was still pretty pissed at Daddy for getting remarried so soon after Mother's death. And I said something about it to one of the old biddies she used to golf with out at the country club.

"And Mother's friend just looked at me, patted my arm, and said, 'Now, Louise, don't you be so hard on your daddy. He's just a man after all—and you know men aren't strong like we women are. They just cain't stand to be alone, and they cain't take care of themselves the way women can.'"

"Amazing," Sally Ann said. "And this old steel magnolia would probably get the vapors if someone called her a feminist."

"My God," Louise laughed, "she'd rather be labeled a Communist or a Democrat."

"So do you feel any better about your dad's marriage?" Sally Ann asked.

"Not really—but I like telling the story."

"You never give an inch, do you, Louise?"

"Hell, no. Not that you should talk—you're the most stubborn person I know."

"Well, Joe once told me I had the strongest will of anyone he'd ever met, man or woman. He meant it as a compliment . . . at least I think he did."

"You and Joe are lucky you found each other. I can't imagine the two of you with other people."

"I've never met a man except Joe I want to spend any time with," Sally Ann said. "I like eyeing hunky guys and imagining what they'd look like naked, but that's as far as it goes.

"Not that there's much to look at where I work—just a bunch of weedy corporate types with slicked-back hair and no muscles."

Louise sighed heavily. "Sounds like the story of my life—nerds or gays, that's all I ever meet. At least you have your Joe to go home to . . . Well, enough of this," she said as she dislodged the sleepy Othello from her lap and put him on the floor. "How about if I play you the Liszt piece I'm working on for the faculty recital? You'll be my first audience."

"Before you start, I have a story for you. This may make you laugh," Sally Ann said. "You remember when you told me about pi and the Bach preludes? Well I had to go to Chicago on business a while back and I was having lunch with the most pretentiously twitty lawyer who was trying to impress me with his knowledge of music . . . ." She told Louise about the way she had squelched Dan Geist, then added, "to paraphrase Dorothy Parker, you can lead a legal whore to culture but you can't make him think."

Louise snickered. "Good for you—score one for our side."

"Your roses are really pretty," Sally Ann said as Louise turned on the lamp by her baby grand piano, lighting up the crystal vase of pink and white roses standing on the lid.

"Thanks," Louise answered, looking a little shame-faced. "I was feeling kind of low so I bought them for myself."

"Nothing wrong with that," Sally Ann said. "I buy myself little treats all the time, especially when I'm feeling bad about work. There's no point in you or me or anybody sitting on her ass and waiting to get taken care of."

Louise didn't answer with words but instead began playing her piano. Her strong pianist's hands gave life to the crashing chords which reverberated from her living room's plaster walls and filled all of her small rowhouse with Liszt's titanic struggles between his secular and sacred passions.

Sally Ann listened intently to the beautiful, powerful music. She noticed that the piano's vibrations had made a few rose petals fall from their stems into a pool of candle light reflecting in the instrument's dully-gleaming black finish. Sally Ann looked at Louise's absorbed face, then closed her eyes and thought about the gift of friendship.

Only Insight, No Solutions

"I have to say, Sally Ann, that after reviewing your test results and talking to you, you have one of the highest needs for autonomy of any client I've ever counseled." Dr. Green picked up the answer sheet for the Graves profile Sally Ann had taken during her first session.

"Look at this Graves test, at the way your answers jump off the chart in category 7. As we've already discussed, this profile gives insight into a person's need for structure and organization, as well as his or her ability both to work with other people and to consider their needs and feelings. For example, someone who scores highly in category 3 is generally completely out for himself and views the world as a kill or be killed place.

"A person who scores highly in category 4 needs structure, hierarchy and external discipline. That person would be well-suited to a career in the military or in a large, regimented corporation. As another example, someone whose answers are clustered in category 6 dislikes the chain-of-command approach. This individual likes meetings, consensus and group action.

"You, on the other hand, have a personality that's moved beyond the need for external organization and consensus, yet your test answers demonstrate a high ability to respect others' rights. You provide your own internal discipline and structure and I'd guess that you generally don't need group approval to reinforce your decisions. Does that seem accurate to you?"

Sally Ann, intrigued despite herself that her answers to seemingly unrelated questions could give such insight into her personality, said, "Yes. I can't stand being told what to do or having to work under someone else's supervision. I just want someone to give me a file or a project, tell me what needs to be done, then set me loose to do it.

"I also can't stand meetings where everyone sits around blathering for hours before anything gets done. I think that's a complete waste of time. I start crawling the walls after about fifteen minutes—I say what I have to say in as few words as possible and I don't understand why everyone else can't just come to the point, make a decision, and then get back to work."

Dr. Green smiled, then asked, "What does this suggest to you about your current position?"

"I guess my personality isn't suited to working for a large corporation, even if my boss had a normal disposition instead of being the lawyer from hell." Sally Ann sat looking at Dr. Green for a few seconds, then added, "This is really interesting. I always thought Luke was the main problem, but maybe it's the job itself."

"Well, clearly the general counsel's erratic behavior is a major source of stress, but even if he had a more even disposition I doubt if you'd be very happy working in such a structured environment."

"I never really thought about it, but you're right," Sally Ann said thoughtfully. "Even when Luke is out of the office for a week or so, I just sort of tolerate being at work . . . I mean, I always try to do my job to the best of my ability but it always seems just like something I have to do—I never get much satisfaction out of it."

"Why did you choose a corporate position to begin with?"

"Mainly because I wanted regular hours and didn't feel like putting in the 80- and 100-hour weeks that so many big law firms require. I worked my way through law school and was so tired when I graduated that the standard 40- to 50-hour corporate week seemed like it would be a vacation."

She added, "I thought about checking out some of the smaller firms, but I also wanted to avoid the client contact that's such a big part of working for them. I really don't like working with people very much—I can do it but I don't enjoy it."

Green picked up another of Sally Ann's test sheets. "Well, you test as almost a complete introvert. I'm not sure I would have picked up on that just from talking to you—you present yourself in a polished and personable manner."

"It's all an act," Sally Ann said with a sigh. "I can go for hours without speaking but most people think that's rude, so I have to force myself to make conversation."

She added sarcastically, "Does this mean that my personality is seriously defective? I've noticed that news stories about serial killers always describe the suspects as introverted loners—do I score high on the deranged postal worker profile?"

Dr. Green laughed. "Of course not. It's true that many lay people use the term 'introvert' in a negative sense, generally to mean lacking in social skills or kind of nerdy. But that's certainly not the case with you.

"I prefer to explain the introvert-extrovert difference in terms of energy. That is, extroverts get pumped up by interacting with other people but start feeling drained and listless if they have to spend a lot of time alone.

"Introverts, on the other hand, get energized by being alone but start feeling depleted after a lot of contact with other people. This is so even if the introverted person is enjoying the others' company."

Sally Ann said excitedly, "That's amazing. I used to think that there was something wrong with me because I get so exhausted after being with a lot of people. I have to go off and be in a room by myself to recharge my batteries."

"There's nothing 'wrong' with being an introvert or 'right' about having an extroverted personality. They are just two different kinds of character traits."

Green added, "Unfortunately for you, though, about 75 percent of Americans have extroverted tendencies and our culture rewards people with outgoing personalities. In Japan, though, the opposite is true—around 75 percent of the Japanese are introverts and inwardness is considered a virtue."

"Since I don't live in Japan, is there anything I can do to make myself more extroverted?" Sally Ann asked. "I don't believe I'll pack up and move to the Orient, especially since I can't stand sushi."

"People can learn coping skills as you've done," Dr. Green replied. "You've learned to present yourself in a more outgoing manner, just as an extroverted person can learn to cope with periods of isolation. But the basic introvert-extrovert trait generally doesn't change."

"So where does this leave me in practical terms, so far as my career is concerned?" Sally Ann asked.

Dr. Green sighed. "Well, I have to say that many of the alternative careers that are easy for lawyers to move to, such as investment banker, are either too structured or involve too much interaction with other people for you. I'm not saying that you couldn't do them— you're intelligent enough to master virtually any career. But I think you'd be just as unhappy in those positions as you are in your current job."

Seeing the look of dismay on Sally Ann's face, Green added, "My opinion is that you're really best suited to working for yourself, and that this should be your ultimate goal. Since your present position is so stressful, you'd probably be well off to find another interim job, but ultimately I think you'll have to be your own boss."

"Great," Sally Ann said glumly. "You tell me I have a lousy personality, I'm not suited to do the job I'm trained for, and I won't be happy doing anything else. Since I'm not a trust fund baby and need to earn some money, where does that leave me?"

Green's face flushed slightly. "First, I did *not* say you have a lousy personality. I said that American culture doesn't generally reward introverts. Considering the state of the popular culture, I consider it a mark of distinction to be out of step.

"So far as earning a living is concerned, virtually no one has the perfect job. There's a big difference between what you *can* do and what you'll be *happy* doing. Most people have to make trade-offs and find the job that will irritate them the least."

Sally Ann said quietly, "You know, when I graduated from law school, I was really proud. I really felt like I'd achieved something."

She added, "I worked my ass off to get through school. Eighty— and 100-hour weeks were common by the time I went to class, worked my job, took care of my house and husband, and helped out my folks . . . Then, when I got out of school, I had one crappy job after another, but I kept thinking things would get better, that there would be a payoff for all my hard work.

"It just kind of makes me sick to think that maybe it was all for nothing." She sat back in her chair, twisting her fountain pen through her fingers.

"I think that most of my clients have similar feelings," Dr. Green said gently. "It's very difficult to invest your time, energy and money in something that proves to be unsatisfactory."

He added, "But I don't think you should view it as having been fruitless. If nothing else, you've proved to yourself that you're capable of setting and reaching extremely high goals. You've also proved that you're capable of holding down a series of responsible jobs. I mean, the work dissatisfaction has always been on your part, not your employers', right?"

"That's true," Sally Ann said. "People generally like and respect my work. My bosses have always been pretty upset when I've quit and moved on. And when I resign from my present position I think Luke will be really unhappy.

"But I have to say that all that intellectual satisfaction is kind of cold comfort emotionally. I was brought up to distrust and disdain emotion, but I'm at a point in my life where I'd like to feel good about something . . . besides my marriage, I mean. My relationship with my husband is my one success in life."

Dr. Green looked at the bare ring finger on his left hand and said sadly, "If I were you, I'd try to take a lot of comfort from that." He started to add something but was interrupted by a nyuk-nyuk-nyuk sound coming from the reception area.

"What's that?" Sally Ann asked. "Is your assistant watching TV?"

Green laughed. "No. She's programmed her computer to do a Three Stooges laugh when she makes a mistake. At least that's the prompt for today—yesterday it was jungle sounds. I never know what she's going to do from day to day."

"My PC at work doesn't have audio capacity," Sally Ann said. "If it did, I'd program my computer to make dive-bombing noises and then push the sound button every time Luke starts yelling at someone."

Dr. Green stood up. "Well, on that note, our time is up so I think we need to quit for today. Shall I schedule you in for the same time next week?"

"All right." Sally Ann didn't know if it was worth the expense to see Dr. Green for many more sessions, since he didn't seem to have any concrete solutions for her problems, but decided to talk the situation over with Joe before making her decision. "I'll see you next week."

She stopped by the assistant's desk on her way out of Green's office, saying, "I like your sound effects."

The woman smiled. "Anything to lighten up the work day."

When Sally Ann got back to her office, she stopped by the ladies' room before going to her cubicle. Karen was standing morosely by the built-in vanity shelf and mirror, breathing heavily and putting makeup over the lumpy red blotches that disfigured her usually smooth complexion.

"Have you got hives again?" Sally Ann asked with alarm. "What's Luke done now?"

"He got mad at me because one of the operating departments gave me the wrong information and I included it in a contract. He said that heads were going to roll and then went storming off the floor."

"Business as usual, I see," Sally Ann said sarcastically.

"It's worse," Karen said, trying not to start crying. "When he was screaming at me he said that the company is probably going to be downsizing and the Legal Department won't be immune from the cuts. What will I do if I lose my job?"

"Can I volunteer to be fired?" Sally Ann thought with glee. She looked at Karen's woeful face and said gently, "I think Luke is just throwing his weight around like he always does. With your skills I think you'd be the last person Luke would let go."

She pulled her comb out of her purse and ran it through her hair. "Besides, if the worst happened, you've been with the company long enough you'd have to get a pretty handsome severance package. Not that it will come to that," she added hastily as a tear rolled down Karen's face.

"It's not the money," Karen said, trying to control her voice. "We have savings and could get by on my husband's salary until I found something else."

"So what are you so worried about, then?" Sally Ann asked.

"What will I do if I lose my job? How will I respect myself? Who will I be?" She sniffled as a tear ran down her face.

"You'll still be yourself," Sally Ann said, dumbfounded that Karen put so much stock in her employment. "More importantly, you'll still have yourself. And you'll still have your health, your skills, your husband and children."

Karen, crying openly, sobbed, "I know I should take comfort from that. But I can't right now. I feel like if I get fired I'll be nothing."

Sally Ann awkwardly patted Karen's shoulder. "Look, it's mid-afternoon. Why don't you take the rest of the day off—go home, put your feet up and relax? I'll get your purse and briefcase so you won't have to go back to the department, and I'll let Luke and Claudia know."

"I'm too scared to take any time off," Karen said shakily as she reached into her pocket and pulled out a small prescription bottle. "I guess it's time for some Xanax."

"Did you get those from your mom?" Sally Ann asked.

"Yes. I've been so keyed up lately that I can't calm down and I've been having trouble sleeping. So Mother gave me these—I try not to take the pills very often but lately I've been craving them all the time."

And you'd rather be zoned out on tranquilizers and working for Luke instead of losing your job? Sally Ann thought, realizing that most of her co-workers probably felt the same way. I guess I really am completely out of sync. But she said nothing, instead wetting a paper towel with cold water and giving it to Karen so she could press it against her face.

"I'm feeling better," Karen said a few minutes later. "Guess I'll go back to work." She paused, then added awkwardly, "Thanks for staying in here with me."

Sally Ann and Karen left the restroom. Two women from another department looked at them with mild curiosity, although tear-stained Legal Department personnel weren't an unusual sight on that floor.

As they walked down the hall toward their cubicles, Luke passed them. Having vented his rage on someone else, he looked relaxed and in control. Sally Ann gave him a glare that would have melted diamonds; Luke had the grace to look away.

"Let me know if I can get you a glass of water or a cup of coffee," Sally Ann said as Karen entered her work station.

Sally Ann went to her own desk, her body tight with tension. She saw a file in her in-basket with a note in Luke's handwriting attached. 'Excellent work,' Luke had written after reviewing her analysis of a complicated legal problem.

Oh fuck you, Luke, Sally Ann thought nastily. Tomorrow or next week you'll be praising Karen and threatening to fire me. She sat down and pulled her guide to the Florida Keys out of a desk drawer. She pressed herself more deeply into her comfortably-upholstered desk chair and read about Key West while another day in the Legal Department droned to its conclusion.

Chapter Six

Seminal Moments

One in Ten Billion

Sally Ann stared in disbelief at the front of the conference room. One of the two men who had been giving a motivational talk to the company's officers had suddenly pulled a rubber skull cap over his dark curly hair. "I'm Mr. Sperm Man," he yelled as he started to run in agitated circles around the second speaker.

"What have we been talking about?" the second man shouted to the group of dark-suited executives. "Overcoming odds . . . ? Competing in a tough market . . . ? Well let me tell you no one encounters worse odds than a single sperm cell trying to get to the ovum of his choice! The odds against any given sperm reaching the egg are astronomical! But obviously conception does take place, or none of us would be sitting here today!

"So when you get discouraged, when you think the barriers are too high and you as one person can't do anything—remember Mr. Sperm Man here! If he can do it, so can you!" Holding out a white scarf with a big red oval in its middle, the man yelled, "Come on, Mr. Sperm Man! Let's see you do it! Come on and pierce this egg!"

Lowering his head, Mr. Sperm Man charged the scarf several times as his partner waved the cloth like a demented toreador. Finally he butted his skullcapped head into the red oval.

"All right Mr. Sperm Man! You did it! What do you say, group?"

"Goal!" a voice shouted from the back of the room.

My life has just hit a new low, Sally Ann thought, discreetly looking from side to side to gauge the reactions of her fellow corporate drones. Most looked embarrassed, but a few of the younger men were laughing.

As Luke had threatened, the company had recently gone through a wave of layoffs, more to follow the '90s downsizing trend than because its finances required the terminations. Mr. Marks had then personally engaged the two speakers, who were making the rounds of all the regional corporations, to give their presentation to his demoralized managers.

Despite her fervent prayers, Sally Ann had not been laid off. I don't believe this, she thought glumly as Mr. Sperm Man pulled off his skullcap and Ovum Man folded the scarf. I can't even get fired from this place.

She had been happily discussing with Joe how the combination of her expected severance pay and unemployment benefits would tide them over until she found another job when the blow fell. Luke had called the members of his legal staff into the Legal Department conference room. He had shut the flimsy door, which gave no privacy whatsoever since the room's padded linen walls were portable and didn't reach the ceiling, then stood looking gravely at his employees.

Oh boy, Sally Ann had thought. This is it! We're all going to get laid off. Oh thank God!

"Well, I have some good news for you people," Luke had said abruptly. "As you know most of the departments in this company are cutting their staff by ten to 20 percent.

"I'm happy to say, though, that the Legal Department won't be losing any people although we won't be able to replace anyone who leaves. I persuaded Mr. Marks that we could save the cost of at least two of your salaries by keeping more of the company's legal work in-house instead of farming it out to private law firms.

"So we'll all be working harder, but we've all still got jobs," Luke had finished.

Sally Ann had sat in stunned silence while the other lawyers almost cried with relief. Goddammit, Luke, she had thought, why did you suddenly have to turn into a human being? She realized the enormous battle Luke must have waged with Mr. Marks to keep his lawyers' jobs.

As many times as you've threatened to fire us, why the hell couldn't you let me go? Sally Ann had silently asked Luke. Then it dawned on her that all along Luke's threats had only been empty blusters used to control and intimidate his staff.

Now, a week later, she sat in another windowless conference room watching a skullcapped jackass and his partner simulate conception. Sally Ann had always thought Mr. Marks was a bit odd, considering his penchant for having polka music played over the building's white-sound system and his habit of assembling the company's officers in the atrium while he addressed them, Mussolini-like, from the balcony outside his office—but having Sperm Man and his sidekick speak to the company's managers went beyond odd.

"You, lady with the pearl necklace . . . what do you say?" Sally Ann realized that Ovum Man was talking to her. Having failed to get anyone to respond to his request for comments, he was selecting unwilling participants from his audience.

Sally Ann stood, thinking that she would have worn a longer skirt if she'd known in advance about this debacle. "Well, I'm a member of this company's legal staff," she said smoothly. "As you know, it's been asked what's the difference between a lawyer and a sperm cell."

Sally Ann paused, then said with a smile, "The difference is that, unlike an attorney, a sperm has a one in ten billion chance of becoming a human being. So I guess that my fellow lawyers and I face even more of an uphill battle than most of you folks in this room."

She sat down gracefully as the men laughed. Sally Ann saw that Karen was glowering at her, undoubtedly upset by the favorable reaction she had gotten from the company's senior managers.

Oh, lighten up, chickie, Sally Ann thought, disgusted by Karen's relentless and ruthless campaign to save her job over the past weeks. She recognized that the company's downsizing called for discreet brownnosing by anyone interested in staying employed, but Karen's servile toadying had gone beyond the pale.

As many verbal blow jobs as you've given Luke and Mr. Marks lately, you'd have nothing to worry about even if I were competing with you, which I'm not. But you'll never see it that way. As paranoid as you are, you've probably at least considered going from flattering words to getting down on your knees and really sucking up . . . Assuming, that is, that anyone around here wants head from an elephant. She smothered a grin, thinking of Joe's Elephant Woman routine in which, pretending to be Karen, he would snort and paw the floor while saying, "Dammit, I am not an elephant—I am an attorney!"

Joe and Sally Ann both suspected that Karen's anti-layoff crusade had degenerated into a slander campaign against her co-workers. Rumors had recently cropped up about Greg and Paul's friendship. The two unmarried young men, who ate lunch together every day and frequently socialized after work, were now thought to be lovers by many people who worked on the Legal Department's floor. Since Mr. Marks was openly homophobic, Sally Ann knew that the CEO would have strongly pressured Luke to get rid of one or both of them if the gossip had come to his attention.

Sally Ann also thought that Karen was spreading nasty stories about her. She had noticed recently that some of the middle-aged and very conservative clerical workers on her floor, who had always seemed to resent her for being a young female manager, had gotten even more surly.

She had always thought that these secretaries were female Uncle Toms, upset that an upstart young lawyer had gotten around the company's carefully-structured hierarchy in which, until a few years ago, there had been "men's" and "girls'" jobs. Although Karen also had a "man's" job, the old bags had never resented her the way they did Sally Ann, probably because the blowsy, overweight Karen didn't threaten them personally, nor did her conservative political and religious views antagonize them.

Sally Ann, who was a libertarian as far as most social issues were concerned, was militantly pro-choice and had often argued the abortion issue with Karen, but had never discussed her beliefs outside the Legal Department. Recently, she had heard muttered epithets on several occasions as she walked past the women, the ringleader of whom was so anti-abortion that every day she wore a lapel pin shaped like metal fetus feet in addition to the gold cross that each of her cronies also wore.

For whatever reason, the dumpy secretaries who wouldn't dare say anything directly to Sally Ann's face had gotten more openly cold and snotty, thus giving her yet another reason to dread coming to work. Sally Ann knew but couldn't prove that Karen was somehow responsible.

After Sperm Man and his sidekick finally released their audience, Sally Ann stopped by the cafeteria to get some iced tea. She saw that Karen and Claudia were huddled together at a table in the otherwise-empty room. Deciding to confront the elephant head on, Sally Ann walked up to her co-workers. "What's going on, ladies?" she asked brightly.

"You look tired, Claudia," she added. "Do you feel all right?"

Claudia, who did look tired and out of sorts, said wearily, "My husband woke me up at 3:00 a.m. and said he had an SRH."

"What's an SRH?"

"Sperm retention headache," Claudia answered grumpily.

"I hope you gave him a real headache for bothering you in the middle of the night," Sally Ann said with a laugh.

"I told him we couldn't do anything since I'd run out of jelly for my diaphragm . . . Then he started bugging me for . . . well, you know, the oral stuff." Claudia turned bright red as she looked away from Sally Ann's amused face.

"And . . . ?" Sally Ann asked, hoping that Claudia had told her cloddish husband to put it on ice until a decent hour.

Claudia said indignantly, "I told him that we are Christian people and I will never do that. So he got mad and slept on the couch for the rest of the night."

Probably went to the bathroom and jerked off, Sally Ann thought. "What does being Christian have to do with oral sex?" she asked, surprised at Claudia's unexpected prissiness.

"Sally Ann," Claudia exclaimed. "I can't believe you'd say that."

Sally Ann looked at the smirking Karen and realized she'd just added another story to Karen's arsenal. Oh screw you, chubby, she thought sourly, realizing that the tenuous bond between them had completely snapped.

"So, what did you think of the presentation, Karen?" Sally Ann asked with false sincerity.

"Um ... I thought it was interesting," Karen replied uncomfortably.

"Yes, it was certainly interesting," Sally Ann said, looking intently at Karen. "Many interesting things have been happening around here lately, haven't they, Karen? Have you heard all the interesting stories that are circulating?"

She kept her eyes on Karen's, smiling blandly as Karen uneasily looked away. "Well, I guess I'll head back to work. See you upstairs, girls." Sally Ann strolled with apparent nonchalance out of the cafeteria and toward the elevators, thinking that she was now completely isolated in the Legal Department.

"I Never Said It To Their Faces"

"This is unbelievable, Joe." Sally Ann laid down the newspaper. "Just as I'm really getting psyched to do an all out job search, I have to read this."

"What's that, babe?" Joe mumbled through a mouthful of pasta with Sally Ann's homemade tomato-basil sauce.

"Right here on the front page of the Inquirer is a story about a woman lawyer who's suing one of the big Center City law firms for sex discrimination."

"So? Sex discrimination suits happen all the time. What happened—she didn't make partner?"

"She says she was passed over for promotion—but that's not what's pissing me off. The paper says her case has come to trial and that yesterday evidence was presented that the firm's managing partner routinely called his female lawyers 'cunts.'"

"What a low-rent scumbag," Joe said. "Did the guy admit it?"

Sally Ann scanned the article. "The Inquirer says the man's defense was, 'I never said it to their faces.'"

"I guess that's why he's getting sued for discrimination instead of sexual harassment," Joe said. "What an asshole."

"Reading garbage like this about one of the most prestigious law firms in this city really depresses me," Sally Ann said. "It certainly doesn't get me up for an extensive job search."

"Well, you know what I keep saying, babe ... if things get too bad, just quit." Joe forked in a huge mouthful of pasta, then dropped a piece of buttered roll to the begging Bubba.

Sally Ann didn't say anything, mainly because she couldn't make Joe understand the ambivalence she felt about her career. She was miserable and doubted whether a job change would do more than temporarily improve her situation; but, as she had told Dr. Green, the thought of walking away from a career she had struggled so hard to achieve made her feel like a failure.

"I'll tell you something else, Sally," Joe said. "I've always tried to stand back and let you fight your own battles, since that's what you said you wanted. But if any bastard ever calls you a cunt I'm going to smash his teeth down his throat."

"I'll probably let you do it." Sally Ann smiled at her vision of Joe beating the tar out of a wormy little lawyer. "Most of those guys are classic bullies—they'd wet their pants if someone actually laid a hand on them.

"Of course," she added, "you know that if you ever hit one of those jerks you'd get slapped with an immediate lawsuit, and the guy would probably show up in court wearing a full body cast."

Joe shrugged as he served himself a large helping of salad. "Look, Mom, I'm eating my greens," he said, smiling at his wife who was convinced he'd die of malnutrition if she wasn't around to cook for him.

"Good. That should stave off a vitamin deficiency for at least one more day . . . I sometimes think that if you were on your own you'd live on cornflakes and microwave pizza."

"Don't forget powdered-sugar doughnuts—one of the essentials of a balanced diet.

"I guess you're stuck with Bubba and me, Sally—it's your mission in life to take care of us poor males." Joe dropped another bite of roll into Bubba's open mouth.

Sally Ann laughed at the sight of her fat little dog standing on his hind legs, his front paws on Joe's knees, as he opened his mouth like a baby bird waiting for the next handout. "To tell you the truth, I'd probably live on tea and toast if you two weren't around. I'd never bother cooking a meal just for myself."

"See—we need each other. I keep you from starving and you keep me from bloating up on junk food."

"The perfect marriage." Sally Ann stood up and walked around the table. She kissed the top of Joe's head and then wrapped her arms around his broad shoulders. Joe leaned back, relaxing his head and shoulders into her torso. Sally Ann bent forward, pressing her warm breasts into the top of her husband's head.

Joe muttered with pleasure. "Would you mind staying there all night?"

Sally Ann felt several fierce head butts at the back of her knees as the jealous Bubba tried to get her attention. "Sister Mary Bubba is coming between us," she said as she straightened up.

"That dog should be approved by the Catholic Church as a form of natural birth control," Joe said grumpily. "He does his best to keep the two of us from ever touching each other."

"I notice you manage to sneak in a feel every once in a while." Sally Ann bent over and patted Bubba who moved away, then looked expectantly up at the table. "You greedy little shit," she said with amusement. "I'm talking about Bubba—not you, Joe. Look at him. Mr. Piggy doesn't want affection, he wants food."

"He's a walking stomach." Joe stood up and started to clear the table.

Sally Ann put the leftover pasta into a covered plastic bowl and then stuck it in the refrigerator. She left Joe to finish loading the dishwasher with Bubba's help.

Sitting in her big, overstuffed leather chair in the study, Sally Ann picked up a detective novel she was reading. The book was one in a series about a south Louisiana cop, a brooding, violent man with a drinking problem. From the author's descriptions of his character's problems, Sally Ann thought that clearly the fictional policeman had a depressive illness that he masked with alcohol and action.

Too bad he doesn't get some treatment for his depression, she thought. But Dave Robicheaux on Prozac would obviate the need for the author's continued examination of his alter ego's dark side, and thus the series would end. Sally Ann smiled, thinking that there would be little for the writer to say about a happy, stable man whose neurotransmitters were chemically balanced. She started to read and was soon lost in the book's moody, atmospheric descriptions of a violent Louisiana world.

Joe and Bubba came into the room and parked themselves on the leather couch. Joe looked fondly at his wife, amused by the fact that she was wearing jeans, one of his old sweaters, and her everyday pearls, an inexpensive necklace he'd given her before he saved up the money to buy the lovely double strand of pearls that was his tenth wedding anniversary gift to her.

Joe stretched out with his head on one armrest and his feet hanging over the other one with Bubba curled up on his chest and stomach. He used the remote to click on the television, then watched the news on CNN.

Sally Ann read, Bubba snored, Joe watched television. As far as all three were concerned, it was a perfect evening.

Tree Burgers, Ex-Heterosexuals and Neo-Suburbanites

"So, what's your sister doing these days?" the assistant Attorney General asked Sally Ann, whom he was interviewing for an entry-level position on his staff.

"Which one?"

"I meant Laurie Ann," he said. Jeff Carmichael and his many brothers had attended the same Catholic high school as Sally Ann and her sisters, a place where, owing to the number of huge Catholic families whose numerous offspring were students there, the same names appeared in the student register year after year. Sally Ann often thought that St. Jude's had spawned dynasties rather than graduates.

"She goes by Laurie now. She said that Laurie Ann sounds too perky, and that our mother's giving three of her daughters the same middle name makes us sound like the Catholic drill team from hell."

Sally Ann added, "Laurie has sort of disconnected herself from the family. The last I heard she was running an art gallery in Santa Fe with her lover."

Carmichael, who'd had a huge and unrequited crush on Laurie Ann for years, sat up straighter behind his desk. "Laurie's not married anymore?"

"Laurie's not a heterosexual anymore," Sally Ann answered. "After her fifth divorce, she decided all her marriages had failed because she'd really been a dyke all along." Sally Ann didn't add that, as usual, Laurie hadn't acknowledged that her marital failures might have owed more to her inordinate self-absorption than to her sexual orientation.

Jeff Carmichael looked shocked, no doubt considering the lively young girl he remembered committing what were still proscribed sexual acts in over half the states. "Dyke?" he finally and weakly said. "That's not very politically correct language."

"Well, Laurie is so p.c. I have to go to the other extreme to counterbalance her. Besides, I don't think she's really a lesbian—I think she just didn't know what to do after her last divorce so, since gay women are currently chic, she thought she'd try girls."

"Jeez," Carmichael said. "Is your mother really upset?'

"I don't think so. When it comes to Laurie, Mother's gotten basically shock-proof. Whenever her name comes up, Mom just shrugs and smokes a cigarette."

"Your mom was always so cool," Jeff said admiringly. "I was really glad to hear she'd remarried. How's that working out?"

"So far so good," Sally Ann answered. "My step-father is a really nice man and I think they're quite happy together. I just wish Al could get my mother to quit smoking—but the most he could do was persuade her to switch from unfiltered Pall-Malls to one of the lighter brands."

"Is your step-father a lawyer like your dad was?" Carmichael asked.

"God no. Mother traded up when she remarried. Al's a retired carpenter."

Sally Ann shifted her position in Carmichael's uncomfortable visitor's chair, wondering when Jeff would get around to telling her about the job for which she was ostensibly interviewing. She had been in his office for half an hour and so far all they had done was gossip about mutual acquaintances and talk about their families. Mainly Jeff had talked and Sally Ann had listened as he sprang manically from topic to topic without slowing down or giving her a chance to say much. He certainly hasn't changed, she thought with amusement, remembering years ago when he'd telephone for Laurie and then talk for an hour to Sally Ann's mother or anyone else who answered the phone.

"So what's your brother Mike up to these days?" she asked as Carmichael finally slowed for breath after mentioning his brother who had been in Sally Ann's law school class.

"About 300 pounds. My mother's real upset because Mike's dating a divorced woman who's ten years older than he is, and she's got two kids.

"I told her, 'Ma, think about his weight. Once Mike passed 300 he's lucky he found a female who can walk upright who'd have him."

Sally Ann laughed. "Sounds like your family's as messed up as mine."

"Probably worse. I sometimes think that the only thing that's worse than having a family is not having one.

"I don't know what I'll do when I have kids of my own—probably screw them up as bad as my parents did us. Of course, first I have to find someone to be my kids' mother, and I don't know if that's going to happen." Carmichael segued into a lengthy narrative about his many romantic misadventures since he graduated from law school fifteen years ago; his thin face was animated as he talked and talked and talked.

Sally Ann tried not to laugh as he got more and more wound up. She wondered how it was possible for any human being to talk so much and still be interesting since, unlike most monologuists, Carmichael had a sense of humor and, though exhausting, his lengthy speeches were witty and intelligent. She did wonder, though, if she could stand to work for someone who was so talkative, especially since she had gotten used to the death-like stillness of Luke's Legal Department.

Her attention wandered, mainly because her brain couldn't process the unending torrent of words fast enough to keep up with Carmichael's mouth. "You're what—40?" she finally managed to interject into Jeff's flow of words. "I know you've never been married, but have you ever lived with anyone?"

"Once, about five years ago," he answered, a shudder running through his thin, rangy body. "It was awful."

"What happened?"

"Oh, this girl was a lot younger than I am and she just wouldn't let me have any space. She was always wanting to, you know, touch me and be with me and one night I finally just couldn't stand it anymore so I went into the bedroom and was lying in a fetal position on the bed when she came into the room, stood over me, popped her chewing gum and asked, 'Does this mean you want to be alone?'"

"Well, what do you expect when all the girls you date are barely eighteen and have IQs lower than their bra sizes?"

"Yeah, yeah, I know," Carmichael said. "But brains and beauty are usually mutually exclusive." He added, staring openly at Sally Ann's legs, "Present company excepted, of course."

Well, strike this job off my list, Sally Ann thought wearily.

"So, should I ask what your little sister Livvie Ann is doing?" Carmichael asked, still unwilling to talk about the requirements of the position Sally Ann had decided she didn't want anyway. "When she was younger it seems like she was stoned every time I saw her."

"Yeah, Olivia was the original dazed and confused kid. You wouldn't know her now. She married an ex-Marine, lives in the suburbs, and voted Republican in the last election."

"That's unbelievable." Jeff laughed. "Does she work?"

"Actually, she has two part-time jobs, one as a curator at the Philadelphia Museum of Art and one as an adjunct professor at the College of Textiles and Sciences. She has a Ph.D. in art history and, like most educated people these days, has found out that her degree plus two dollars still won't get her a cup of coffee."

"What about your oldest sister, Mariclaire? I never knew her that well. Is she an artist like Laurie and Livvie or a lawyer like you?"

"Neither. By day she's a research chemist, by night she and her husband live an environmentally correct life of rigid self-reliance in a semi-rural area outside of Portland," Sally Ann said. "And she goes by Claire now—she thought Mariclaire was too Catholic."

"So she's left the Church?" Jeff asked, giving "church" an intonation that indicated he, like most Catholics, was capitalizing the word in his mind.

"Claire doesn't go to church any more but she must still need the inflexible structure and unbending rules the Catholic Church used to provide."

"How's that?"

"She's joined the eco-church. I call her St. Claire of the Redwoods when she's being particularly self-righteous. She and her husband follow more rules and regulations than if they were still Catholics."

"Don't you care about Mother Earth?" Carmichael teasingly asked Sally Ann.

"Up to a point, but when being ecologically correct starts interfering with basic hygiene I draw the line."

"What do you mean?"

"I was visiting Claire and her husband out in Oregon a few years ago and they'd decided to go on this huge water conservation binge. At a time, I might add, when there wasn't a drought or water emergency taking place, and even though they're living in the middle of one of the Pacific Coast rainforests.

"So they decided that indoor plumbing was anti-earth and they actually built an illegal outhouse at the back of their property. When I told Claire I thought that was really gross and I intended to keep on using the bathroom she told me haughtily that she and my brother-in-law thought that their shit was a gift to the earth. So I decided to take myself and my gifts to a motel.

"Plus she's got more food rules than an Orthodox rabbi. She keeps an eco-kosher kitchen which means that she won't buy three-fourths of the food that's available because it's processed, has pesticide residues, or was somehow grown or produced in an environmentally incorrect manner. I got so tired of eating tofu casseroles that one night I sneaked out and got a tree burger."

"Tree burger?"

"That's what Joe and I have called one of the fast food chains' hamburgers ever since I got back from that Oregon trip. Claire told me that no environmentally conscious person would ever buy from that company because they use Brazilian beef from cows grazed on cleared rainforest land."

Sally Ann stopped talking and looked at Carmichael who was still giving indiscreet glances at her face and legs. "I don't have any more sisters or mutual friends left to talk about," she said. "Do you want to tell me about this job of yours?"

"Not much to say," Carmichael answered. "I can tell you right now that you're totally over-qualified for the position."

"We both knew that to begin with," Sally Ann said coolly.

"So why are you interested in this job?" Jeff asked.

"Because I'm unhappy in my present position but, the way the job market is, if I want to move on I'll probably need to take a lesser job somewhere else. Your ad says you need someone to write briefs and argue motions in criminal cases. That sounds interesting so I thought I'd send you my resume."

"That about sums it up—my case load has gotten so heavy I need someone to write some of my briefs and go to court when I can't make it."

Carmichael stood up and walked around his desk. "Well, thanks for coming by, Sally Ann. It was great talking about old times. I'll let you know about the job."

Sally Ann realized the 'interview' was over. She had spent over an hour in Jeff Carmichael's office; Jeff had talked about the job for about fifteen seconds. Carmichael hadn't asked her about her work experience or her academic record, nor had he discussed such matters as co-workers, salary, benefits, office hours, or even the types of criminal cases his office handled. She assumed that he had never really been interested in hiring her and had scheduled the appointment just to gossip about the past.

Thanks for nothing, she thought with irritation, annoyed that she had wasted a personal day on the meeting.

Carmichael shook hands with Sally Ann then escorted her to the elevator, talking continually the whole time. He was still talking as the elevator doors closed. Sally Ann waved goodbye and smiled, deciding there was no point in being in a bad mood since she knew she didn't want to work for or with Jeff.

On her way home Sally Ann stopped off at the video store to return Jimmy Buffett's 'Live By the Bay' concert video which she rented at least once a month. As usual, the short Philadelphia cop who hung around the store after his shift ended was there, gossiping with the manager.

The policeman smiled appreciatively at the sight of Sally Ann in her neat dark-blue interview suit, heels and pearls. She smiled politely back, thinking that the man, whose head reached just past her shoulder, looked like a size-challenged storm-trooper in his navy jodhpurs and high leather riding boots. Sally Ann had once overheard two older cops complaining that, although the Police Department's height standards had been lowered so that more women would be eligible for the force, the main people to take advantage of the new rules were short ethnic men. Looking at Officer Santamaria in his jack boots, Sally Ann smiled more broadly; Santamaria, thinking she was flirting with him, puffed out his chest.

"Anything else you want today?" the manager asked as Sally Ann returned the Buffett tape.

"A lottery ticket, please."

The manager ran a ticket off the computer and handed it to Sally Ann. "You know, I'm happy to do business with you but as often as you've rented that concert tape you might as well buy your own copy."

"I would but I haven't been able to find it anywhere. Are you offering to sell me your store copy?" Sally Ann gave the manager five dollars to cover the tape rental and lottery ticket.

The man laughed. "Nope. You're not the only Parrot Head who uses my store. But I could order the tape for you from my distributor."

"That would be great," Sally Ann said. "My husband might get pretty steamed, though. I was watching the video last night and just after the concert promoter yelled, 'Are all you Parrot Heads ready to party?' my husband shouted, 'No, goddammit' and threw the TV Guide against the VCR."

"Yeah, the spouses of you Buffett fans have to put up with a lot."

"Well, maybe this will be the winning lottery ticket and he'll be happy I stopped in to return the tape." Sally Ann filled out her name, address and phone number on the order card the manager handed her.

"You never know," the man said. "When I was working at one of our other stores, I sold a twelve million dollar ticket to one of my regular customers."

"Twelve million?" Sally Ann asked weakly. "Can you imagine what it would be like to win twelve million dollars?"

"Yeah, I can imagine," the manager and Santamaria said in unison. Sally Ann and the men laughed.

"Someday it will be one of us," Sally Ann said.

"Good luck to us all," Santamaria said, waving goodbye to Sally Ann as she left the video store. The manager and he watched Sally Ann with longing as she walked across the parking lot to her car.

Chapter Seven

Ms. Middle-Class Values

"They Should Have Assassinated You"

$\mathcal{W}$hen Luke informed his staff that more of the company's legal work would be kept in-house, he severely understated the situation. Every attorney in the Legal Department was wading through stacks of case files that had been returned to Luke by the distraught managing partners of the law firms from whose annual billings thousands of inflated hours had just been ripped.

The department almost hummed with busyness and purpose as all the lawyers except Sally Ann eagerly attacked their new responsibilities. Sally Ann was working as hard as her colleagues, or possibly even harder considering the two appellate briefs Luke had asked her to rewrite after he'd decided he didn't like the drafts submitted by one of the company's few remaining outside counsel. Unlike her co-workers, though, she wasn't buoyed with relief at still having a job.

This morning Sally Ann sat at her desk answering interrogatories, or written questions about a lawsuit, submitted to her company by the plaintiff in a products liability case. Her employer had no connection to the plaintiff, a factory worker injured by a piece of equipment from which a co-worker had removed a safety guard.

However, the company had made a component part incorporated into the machine by its primary maker.

The injured man was suing the two manufacturers because the workers' compensation laws prevented him from suing his employer, and the employee who had actually removed the safety guard had no assets. As Sally Ann's torts teacher had often told her freshman class in law school, "Always sue the deep pockets defendant—don't sue the guy with holes in his Keep on Truckin' T-shirt."

Sally Ann's company had no moral obligation to the injured man but it did have deep pockets in the form of corporate assets and liability insurance. So Sally Ann sat answering legal questions asking for detailed information about the component product's design and construction. She used information supplied by the company's engineering staff, and later would have one of the engineers review her answers for technical correctness.

I am so bored, she thought, wondering if anyone would notice if she drafted the answers in a parody of a leading author's macho, techno-thriller style. Thinking of the writer's lovingly detailed, almost masturbatory descriptions of men and their machines, she decided that the author already parodied himself, but thought she'd give it a try anyway.

She read Interrogatory No. 12, which demanded: 'State in detail the manner in which Plaintiff was injured.' Instead of typing the correct response into her computer—'This information is outside the scope of this Defendant's knowledge and is solely within the purview of facts known to Plaintiff and his attorney'—Sally Ann began scribbling on a legal pad: 'Plaintiff strode across the factory floor, his broad shoulders straining the seams of his orange coverall. Confident of his young male strength, he approached the massive throbbing machine which pulsated with an energy matched by his own vigor. This is a man's life, he thought, scanning his male co-workers with his keen grey eyes and feeling thankful that his unit had no ball-busting feminist lesbos in it. Although he saw that the safety guard had been removed, Plaintiff knew that the perfect symmetry between himself and the machine's incarnate masculine power could not be breached. He reached out and . . . '

Her telephone rang. "This is Luke, Sally Ann. Please come into my office."

She walked the ten feet from her cubicle into Luke's. "What can I do for you, Luke?" she asked the general counsel, whose desk was, as always, overflowing with files.

"I need you to go to a worker's compensation hearing for me. It starts in 45 minutes. Here's the file." Luke handed the folder to Sally Ann, then gestured dismissively toward his cubicle's opening.

"What position is the company taking?" Sally Ann didn't bother protesting the lack of notice or the fact that she knew nothing about the case; since recalling much of the company's routine litigation files Luke had become even more arbitrary and erratic about dumping work on his staff.

"We won't contest continued compensation payments so long as the injured worker submits to another medical examination by our specialist and the doctor verifies that the man isn't fully rehabilitated. Without the exam, the company will fight paying additional benefits to this employee." Luke gestured again toward the space where the door would have been if his cubicle had been a real office. "Let me know how the hearing goes."

"Okay." Sally Ann left Luke's work station, grabbed her purse and briefcase from behind her desk and started to leave the department. On her way out she passed Karen who was lumbering self-importantly down the corridor to Luke's office. Time for more sucking up, I see, Sally Ann thought; she smiled with false cordiality at the woman who had decided that Sally Ann was now her nemesis in the Legal Department.

"I'm going to a worker's comp hearing, Claudia," Sally Ann said as she passed Claudia's desk. "I should be back after lunch." She saw Claudia write down the information in the log that Luke insisted she keep detailing the whereabouts of everyone in the Legal Department except himself.

Standing in the hall outside her department, Sally Ann looked at her reflection in the polished granite slabs that faced the corridor as she waited for the elevator. As always, she was a little surprised to see an outwardly poised adult woman staring back at her instead of the sad scruffy child she had once been.

When the elevator doors opened, Frank Parsons, Executive Vice President—Marketing, walked out of the paneled compartment. Sally Ann had heard Luke screaming at Parsons several days before; she wondered if he was foolishly going back for round two.

"How are you today, Sally Ann?" Parsons asked with a smile, holding the elevator door open for her.

"Just fine, sir," she answered with apparent cheerfulness. "Luke's sending me to a compensation hearing so I'm on my way to the state office building."

Parsons, a kindly grey-haired man who was liked and respected by his staff, looked at her and said quietly, "Working for Luke is a real bear, isn't it, Sally Ann?"

"You have no idea, sir," she said. "You have no idea."

Parsons released the elevator door. As it closed Sally Ann saw him standing in the hall, just looking at her with an expression of yearning tenderness she often saw on older men's faces.

Why can't I work for someone like Mr. Parsons? she thought as the elevator took her to the first floor. Obvious answer, you moron— because you're a lawyer and all your bosses will be lawyers.

Sally Ann walked the few blocks from her office to the site of the compensation hearing. It was a grey fall day with a raw underbite to the air. She shivered and wished she had worn her trench coat.

Everyone walking past her on the sidewalk looked chilled, closed off and irritable; Sally Ann thought longingly of watching sun on the ocean from the shaded porch of a small beach house. Although the cottage existed nowhere but in her mind, she knew every detail of it, from the riotously blooming tropical plants and cane chairs on the veranda to the blue and white striped sheets in the bedroom. Jimmy Buffett's music played over the sound system; Joe and Bubba sprawled in the hammock taking a nap together as warm breezes blew over them. Sally Ann sat in the shade of a large umbrella in a teak planter's chair, reading a book and completely relaxed.

Thinking that mind over matter was no substitute for a warm coat, she quickly reached the nondescript building on Arch Street that housed the Bureau of Workers Compensation. She went to the hearing room and introduced herself to the claimant and his attorney.

"If your client will undergo a medical exam that verifies his continuing disability, the company won't contest his receiving additional benefits," Sally Ann told the lawyer, a pudgy, balding man named Fred Barnes who wore the cheap suit and anxious expression of many solo legal practitioners.

"Is this acceptable to you?" Barnes asked his client, a young man whose leg had been injured in a factory accident.

"Okay by me," the client said cheerfully.

"Then this hearing should be over in about three minutes—we'll tell the comp judge we've reached an agreement and see if he'll issue an order confirming the deal," Sally Ann said.

They waited at the back of the hearing room for their case to be called. Sally Ann noticed that a number of workers and their lawyers looked upset and disgruntled. She found out why when the clerk read out the name of the next claimant.

"Fifty-five thousand in medical benefits for your damn wrist and now you want more?" the elderly, red-faced administrative law judge exploded. "My God, man, your employer should have had you assassinated instead of paying to fix you up!"

The workman, a beefy man in jeans and red plaid shirt whose right wrist was encased in some kind of surgical steel contraption, turned white. "Um . . . your honor, . . ." his lawyer said helplessly.

"God, I've heard some strange stories about this judge," Barnes muttered to Sally Ann. "I guess they were all true." They waited uneasily for the court clerk to call their docket number.

"So, young man," the judge scowled over his reading glasses at Barnes's client after Sally Ann had explained their agreement, "you still want to keep sucking on the public teat?"

The client blushed with embarrassment and uneasily shifted his weight to lean more heavily on his cane. He tried to speak but couldn't get any words out.

"If I may say, your honor," Sally Ann interjected, "my company doesn't doubt that this employee continues to need medical rehabilitation. This is particularly so since I've had a chance to observe the difficulty the claimant still has in walking.

"We certainly don't think that this young man is malingering. We simply want him to be re-examined by our orthopedic specialist to confirm the degree of his disability. We came into this hearing fully expecting to continue paying for his rehab therapy."

The judge glared at Sally Ann who looked coolly back at him. He shuffled some papers in irritation, then glanced at Barnes, trying to find a reason to demean him. "Well, counselor," the judge asked Barnes sneeringly, "can you say anything—or has this woman cut out your tongue as well as certain other parts?"

Barnes clenched his jaw while Sally Ann struggled to keep from saying something that would get her sanctioned for contempt. "Mrs.

Stanton and I have reached an agreement that protects my client's interests, is acceptable to the employer, and is permitted by law," Barnes finally said in an even monotone, the lack of emotion in his voice effectively conveying his anger.

"Oh, all right," the judge said. "Let the record reflect that claimant shall undergo the requested medical examination within the next fourteen days, compensation benefits to continue, subject to the results of the medical exam, for 90 days from today's date. So ordered." The judge banged his gavel, then said to Barnes, "Draft a written order reflecting my ruling and send it to my clerk for my signature. Dismissed."

Barnes, his client, and Sally Ann left the hearing room as the clerk summoned the next victims to the judge's presence. In the hall Sally Ann shook hands with the two men and told the claimant she hoped his injured leg would continue to improve. "After the judge returns the signed order, I'd appreciate it if you'll send me a copy for my file," she said to Barnes.

"Be glad to," he replied. "Sorry he was such a jerk to you."

Sally Ann shrugged. "He was worse to you."

"Just another day in the legal wars," Barnes said. Had his client not been there, Sally Ann knew Barnes would have had much more to say. As it was, he waved a casual goodbye and walked away with his client, slowing his stride to the young man's limping gait.

Nuked Fruitcakes

Sally Ann walked for blocks through a chilly, dispiriting mist from the Bureau of Workers' Compensation to the Twentieth Street Bar and Grill for a quick lunch. She wanted a bowl of the restaurant's homemade soup and a pot of hot tea to warm her up.

"What's going on with you today?" Aaron asked as he showed Sally Ann to her favorite table, the small one in the corner next to the front window.

"I've just escaped from the clutches of the law," Sally Ann said, shivering as warm air from the radiator enveloped her chilled body.

"Nothing's new with me either," Aaron said. "I guess you'll be having your grey day special—soup and hot tea?"

"I'd order something else just to prove I'm not that predictable but I'm freezing."

Aaron brought Sally Ann a basket of the hard rolls that were delivered daily from a South Philly bakery and her first pot of tea. "What's with all this goat cheese in today's specials, Aaron? You guys aren't getting trendy, are you?"

"Trendy? Goat cheese went out with pesto, yuppies and the '80s, sweetie. The fact that our chef is using it is a clear sign that it's a cliché."

Sally Ann smiled at Aaron who grinned back. "I'll get your soup for you right away—got to warm up my favorite straight white chick."

"That's me," Sally Ann said ruefully. "Ms. Middle-Class Values."

"Got to be who you are, dear." Aaron bustled away toward the kitchen.

I don't know how to be anyone else, Sally Ann thought. Over-achieving, stressed-out and guilt-ridden.

As she passed a music store on her way back to the office, Sally Ann decided to step in for a few minutes. Her Jimmy Buffett 'A-1A' tape, recorded during the singer's early years in Key West, had worn out from overuse and she wanted to replace it with a CD.

"Where's your Jimmy Buffet section?" she asked one of the young clerks, all of whom were androgynous, grungy and in their early twenties.

"Over there," he gestured.

Sally Ann picked out her compact disk, then went to pay for it. The same kid who'd shown her the Buffett section rang up her purchase. He looked curiously at Sally Ann, who was wearing a tailored grey dress, an ivory cardigan, and pearls. "Are you, um, like, a Parrot Head?" he finally asked.

"Um, well, yes," she answered, smiling cheerfully at the clerk, who had six earrings in one ear and a nose ring. "You don't approve?" she asked when he grimaced.

"Oh, I guess some of his early stuff isn't bad," he said politely. "But we've got an employee who's a militant Buffett fan. She keeps playing the 'Fruitcakes' CD over the sound system and the rest of us are sick of it. We're thinking about nuking the disk in the store's microwave."

Sally Ann laughed. "You and my husband should get together." She stuffed the CD into her briefcase and left the store, wondering if she could be a proto-slacker and still wear her pearls. A cold drizzle had started to fall so she hurried back to her office.

Escaping From the Clutches of the Law

"Where's Claudia?" Sally Ann asked as she passed the secretaries' work area, in which their lower status in the corporate structure was demonstrated by the waist-high partitions that separated their cubicles.

"Getting her boobs nuked," the recently un-pregnant Annie answered. In defiance of company policy she had pinned several snapshots of her new baby to her cubicle's low padded divider.

"Oh. I forgot it's mammogram day."

"Luke's been looking for you, Sally Ann," Annie said.

"Did he say what he wants?"

"No. But he doesn't seem to be in a very good mood."

"Well, I'll go see what he needs," Sally Ann said with a sigh, thinking that Luke's mood would probably improve with either a lobotomy or a blow job, neither of which she was able or willing to give him. She dropped off her purse and briefcase at her cubicle, then walked around the partition into Luke's office.

"Annie says you're looking for me, Luke."

"Where the hell have you been, Sally Ann?" Luke said in a dangerously quiet voice. She looked at him and saw that his face was red and swollen, and that the veins in his temples were throbbing.

Oh, shit, Sally Ann thought, he's looking totally crazed. She said quietly, "I went to the worker's comp hearing you asked me to attend, Luke. If you'll wait a second I'll go get the file and tell you how it went."

"This is absolutely unacceptable," Luke said furiously, his voice rising.

"I did what you asked me to do, Luke. I don't see what's unacceptable about that." Sally Ann's calm, reasonable voice seemed to enrage the general counsel even more.

"You've been gone two hours, dammit."

"Luke," Sally Ann said patiently, "I told Claudia that I was going to lunch after the hearing. I left the office at 10:45 and walked out of the state building at noon." She looked at her watch, saying, "It's five past one right now. I didn't take more than my allotted hour for lunch."

"You broke the rules, dammit," he snarled.

"I don't understand what the problem is," Sally Ann said, feeling as if she were an unwilling performer in a surreal theater piece.

"The problem is that I'm supposed to know where all members of my staff are at all times."

"And I complied with that, Luke. I told Claudia, the head secretary, where I was going and when I'd be back. And I saw her write it down in her log."

"Well she didn't tell me."

"I'm sorry, Luke, but I don't have any control over what Claudia says or doesn't say to you. You could have checked the log, you know."

"This isn't going to happen again, goddammit. From now on you tell me personally where you're going and when you'll be back."

"I don't think so, Luke," Sally Ann said calmly.

"What the hell do you mean by that?" Luke's face got even more pulpy and swollen.

"I mean that you are so angry you're not thinking clearly. If you'll calm down so that we can talk like two adults, then we'll continue this conversation. Otherwise I'm going back to my desk."

"I'm very unhappy with you, Sally Ann," Luke screamed.

Sally Ann's composure snapped. "Then take a tranquilizer, goddammit," she snapped, her voice quiet but hard with rage.

Luke looked at Sally Ann with astonishment. "I . . ." he started to say.

"Forget it Luke. You just ragged on me one time too many. I'm quitting, effective immediately. I suggest you notify the Human Resources Department that I'm owed two weeks' pay in lieu of notice."

"But I didn't mean it, Sally Ann," Luke whined, looking as shocked as a two year old who's been smacked in the middle of a tantrum.

"Oh fuck you, Luke."

Sally Ann walked quickly back to her desk. She stuffed her framed photos of Joe and Bubba into her briefcase, then grabbed her guide to Key West and Parrot Head handbook and crammed them on top of the pictures. She picked up her purse and briefcase, then walked down the long hall of padded cubicle partitions toward the front of the Legal Department. The other lawyers, who had overheard everything, stared open-mouthed as she strode past their work stations.

"I'll be seeing you, Annie," Sally Ann said as she walked by the young woman's desk. "Take care of yourself and that new baby of yours."

"Where are you going?" Annie asked.

"Anywhere that doesn't have Luke Johnson in it."

Sally Ann went to the elevators. Out of the corner of her eye she saw Luke hurrying out of the Legal Department toward the executive suites and Mr. Marks's office. The polished walnut doors opened and she stepped into the elevator.

At the first floor security desk, she signed out, writing her name and time of departure in the building's log. In the 'estimated time of return' column, she printed in block capitals, "Ms. Middle-Class Values is taking a permanent hike."

"See you, Mr. Price," Sally Ann said to the elderly man behind the security desk. "I'll never have to look at this hideous red and purple rug again."

"Lucky you," Price said. "I see it in my dreams."

Sally Ann walked out of the building into the cold rain, then turned toward the parking lot where she had left her car.

Chapter Eight

No Snivelling

A Buffett Epiphany

After walking out on Luke and her job, Sally Ann was surprised that the decision she'd agonized over for months had been made so quickly and for such a comparatively trivial reason—Luke had thrown one tantrum too many and she just couldn't take it anymore.

She felt a mixture of anger, anxiety, relief and guilt. Despite his constant offers that she could quit, Joe was upset although he tried not to show it. Sally Ann knew that he worried about making the mortgage payments without using up her 401(k) funds. She was annoyed with him, and annoyed with herself for feeling guilty.

Lying sleepless in bed in the early morning hours when the sickening anxiety struck, Sally Ann would stare through the dark at the ceiling as her throat and stomach muscles knotted up from tension. She wondered miserably if she had screwed herself, her career and her marriage.

She would get angry at Joe as he lay snoring beside her, unreasonably angry that he had always been treated well in his various jobs and had never fully understood the strain of working for Luke. She got more angry at her family, for the unfair demands they had made on her and the fact that they had bled her dry, physically and emotionally. She was angry at herself, for having given in to everyone else's unwarranted demands for so many years.

Night after night the same thoughts poured endlessly through her mind. She coped as well as she could, never waking Joe or asking for comfort. Usually after an hour or two the anxiety would loosen its grip on her; her muscles would relax and she would go back to sleep until Joe's alarm went off and both of them awoke. Joe never knew the silent battles his wife had been fighting with herself and her fear, and Sally Ann never told him.

Two days after she quit Gary Miller, her former employer's Vice President—Human Resources (or what was once called the personnel manager), telephoned Sally Ann at home. He told her that Mr. Marks wanted her to come back.

"He's very upset that you left, Sally Ann," Miller said. "You are so well-regarded around here and Mr. Marks had hoped that, as one of our women executives, your career would expand beyond the Legal Department."

"Well no one ever told me that," Sally Ann said. "Besides, for the foreseeable future I'd still be working for Luke and I just can't take that anymore."

"Well, Sally Ann, Mr. Marks and I had no idea that the situation in the Legal Department was so bad. If you had just spoken up perhaps we could have done something."

"I did speak up," Sally Ann retorted, "and so did Karen Brennan. You may recall that after the Christmas party fiasco last year Karen sat in your office and cried for over an hour. Then you called me down to corroborate Karen's story and I did.

"And both of us spoke to you again, at length, several months ago. We told you about Luke's mood swings, his rages, his inappropriate comments, the fact that he can't delegate authority— we told you about everything that was going on. And as I recall, Avery Weinstock came in as we were leaving to make his own complaint about Luke.

"Plus, I've been told that at every senior managers' meeting for the last two years people have griped about Luke and the way he's running the Legal Department into the ground.

"So don't try to tell me that you and Mr. Marks didn't know what was going on," Sally Ann concluded with quiet force in her voice.

"Well, I'm sorry you feel so strongly about this," Miller said with oily insincerity. "I have to tell you that you're walking away from a job that many lawyers would give their eyeteeth to have."

"More power to them," Sally Ann said. "And I'm telling you something else, Gary. I'm going to file for unemployment benefits and if the company contests my claim I'll go to the EEOC and file a sexual harassment charge against the company."

"On what grounds?" Miller spluttered with indignation.

"On the ground that Luke's constant sexual comments and fecal references were directed toward his women staffers, including me, for purposes of creating a hostile and intimidating workplace. As you know, such actions constitute harassment that the company is obligated to stop once it has notice of the occurrence. Karen and I, along with several of the secretaries, talked to you and your assistant about this but nothing was done to Luke and nothing changed. So the company is now in the position of having condoned Luke's actions."

"But Sally Ann," Miller said patronizingly, "Luke creates an environment that's hostile and intimidating for everyone, not just you ladies."

"This is true. But, as you know, generally being an asshole isn't against the law," Sally Ann replied coolly. "Fortunately for me, I fall into a protected category and Luke's behavior is legally proscribed as it relates to me. And I intend to take advantage of that fact."

"Goddamn, you play hardball," Miller said with reluctant admiration in his voice.

"It's too bad it had to come to this," Sally Ann said. The conversation ended; aside from sending her various forms to fill out in connection with releasing her 401(k) and vested retirement funds, Sally Ann heard nothing else from her former employer.

When it wasn't 3:00 a.m. and she wasn't eaten up with anxiety, Sally Ann knew she had made the right decision in refusing to go back. Had Luke not been so awful, she knew she would have put up with the slow death of working a corporate law job simply because the money and the prestige were too hard to walk away from. Even finding out from Dr. Green that she wasn't suited to working in any highly structured environment hadn't been enough to make her give up the security of an outwardly comfortable job.

Her epiphany came one evening as Bubba and she waited for Joe to get home from work. They were sitting on the couch listening to a Jimmy Buffett tape when Sally Ann started paying attention to the lyrics of 'Growing Older But Not Up'—"I'd rather die while I'm living than live while I'm dead," she sang along with Jimmy.

"That's it, Bubba," she said. "I paid thousands of dollars to Dr. Green for insight that was already available to me on this tape. If I keep on working standard jobs, even if a normal person and not Luke is my boss, I'll stay trapped in a living death. This is my chance to live for myself, for the first time in my life."

She added, "Don't worry, sweetie. You'll still have all the dog biscuits you can eat. Joe will see to that."

Bubba looked wisely at Sally Ann and licked her hand. "You want to know how I can justify being taken care of financially? Well, I'm not comfortable with it—I've been earning my own money since I was sixteen and I hate the thought of depending on Joe.

"But I'm just going to have to live with the situation for a while. I think this is a test, Bubba. I've never really trusted anybody—I came as close to trusting Joe as I thought I could but there was always a part of me holding back, hedging my bets. I liked knowing that I had my own career and would never be stuck like my mother was.

"I think I was always afraid that if I didn't bring in money, Joe might treat me the way my dad acted toward my mother. So now for the first time I have to completely trust my husband the way he trusts me. It's going to be really hard but I have to do it."

Bubba rolled over on his back so that Sally Ann could rub his warm fat stomach. Sally Ann heard the front door open; Joe yelled hello.

"What are you two doing?" Joe asked, looking at his wife and dog together on the couch in their matching outfits. Sally Ann wore a bright tropical print blouse and shorts; Bubba had an even brighter floral bandanna around his neck. His little straw hat lay on the couch beside him.

"Bubba's turned into a Parrot Dog," Sally Ann said fondly as she put the hat on top of her dog's head. "He wants us to take him to Key West and the original Margaritaville Café."

"It's two weeks before Thanksgiving and you're wearing beach clothes, Sally."

"But in my mind it's 75 degrees and sunny."

"You have infinite patience, Bubba," Joe said as the dog put his head on his front paws and sighed. The straw hat slipped to one side so Sally Ann righted it. "What am I going to do with you, Sally?"

"A kiss would be nice." Joe complied, bending over his wife and kissing her lightly on the lips. Then he sat down next to her, breathing out heavily and loosening his tie.

"Hard day?" Sally Ann asked, feeling slightly guilty that at 8:00 p.m. she was still relaxed and refreshed while her husband was clearly beaten down by his day.

"Not so much hard . . . mainly just long."

"Well, I've got dinner in the oven. We can eat whenever you want."

"You don't have to wait for me, Sally. I don't mind if you go ahead and eat before I get home."

"I know . . . but I want to wait. I like being with you and I know you don't care for eating alone."

The three of them sat together in comfortable silence for a few minutes. Joe was so tired he didn't even pick up the remote and start scanning the TV channels. Sally Ann patted Bubba with one hand and stroked Joe's leg with the other. Joe started to relax, then dozed off.

Sally Ann sat between her snoozing husband and dog. Suddenly one of the fits of weepiness that had been plaguing her since her resignation struck; she got tears in her eyes and clenched her jaw tightly to keep from crying.

Sally Ann's father, who had equated all expressions of female emotion with incipient mental illness, had punished his children when they wept and squelched all outward signs of their rare happiness. When she was a young girl, there had been several times when, overwhelmed with the sadness and loneliness she felt as a result of her mother's mental illness, Sally Ann had locked herself in the bathroom and cried. Sitting on the side of the bathtub with the water running, she had stuffed a towel in her mouth to muffle her sobs so that her father and sisters wouldn't hear her weeping. But such occasions had been rare.

She had learned at an early age generally to control her feelings, and contemptuously thought of crying as one of the most overrated human activities. Her few experiences with it generally left her feeling exhausted, weak and ashamed; she never experienced the emotional relief and uplift that all the self-help books promised to men who got in touch with their 'feminine' side.

Quit crying, stupid, Sally Ann thought fiercely. She wiped her eyes with the back of her hand, then sat with her eyes closed until the tearfulness passed.

"Joe," she whispered, "honey. Wake up and go change your clothes so we can eat dinner."

Joe picked up her hand and sleepily kissed it. Tasting the salty dampness on her skin, he woke up enough to look closely at his wife's face. Sally Ann's complexion was so fair that just getting tears in her eyes was enough to puff up her eyes and redden her nose. Joe put his arm around his wife's shoulders and pulled her close to him. "We'll get through this, babe."

"I feel like I've screwed up everything," Sally Ann said morosely as waves of anxiety flooded her.

"You haven't screwed up. You just decided you weren't going to let Luke shit on you anymore. I'm proud of you, Sally. The other spineless jerks you worked with will still be bitching about Luke the day they retire—you were the only one with backbone enough to make some waves and leave."

"Yeah, but they're spineless jerks with paychecks." A tear rolled down Sally Ann's face and her nose started to water. "Oh, goddammit, now I'm crying again."

"We'll get through this," Joe repeated. "I don't deny I've been worried about money—but we'll manage, especially now that your unemployment claim has been approved."

"What if I'm just a wimp, Joe?"

"What?"

"What if Luke wasn't as bad as I thought? I mean, no one else has quit, so maybe I'm just a weakling who couldn't put up with a tough boss."

"The ones who stay are the wimps, not you, Sally."

"Well if I'm so strong then why do I feel so shitty? One minute I'm on top of the world, the next I'm crying."

"Because you made a hard decision and gave up a lot. Most people couldn't have done that. But you did and I'm proud of you."

"Oh, Joe." Sally Ann pressed her husband's hand to her face. "Well," she said shakily," you'd better hurry up and change your clothes so we can eat or your dinner's going to get burned up." She got to her feet, then leaned over to pick up Bubba's straw hat from the floor.

Joe stood up. Bubba sleepily opened one eye. "Should we wake up the stomach on four legs?" Joe asked.

"His nose will wake him up as soon as I take the chicken out of the oven."

"Then we'll see you in the kitchen, Mr. Piggy," Joe said as he followed his wife out of the room.

Klonopin and Carbohydrates

As holidays go, Thanksgiving that year fell short on the scale of awfulness Sally Ann usually applied to her family's get-togethers. Unlike past celebrations, no one had to leave the dinner table to go vomit from nerves in the bathroom. No one overdosed on pain medication and slumped and dribbled his way through the meal. Contrary to former occasions when the arriving guests found the oven cold and the ham unbaked or the turkey unroasted, there was actually a dinner cooking when Sally Ann and Joe arrived and the table was already set with her mother's good dishes and silver.

But it was still a gathering of the Fitzpatrick family. Olivia sniped at Sally Ann, who had brought the dinner rolls and pies, for not making the bread from scratch. "It's a holiday, Sally Ann," she said petulantly. "Couldn't you have gone the extra mile?"

Sally Ann, who had stayed up past midnight the night before to bake three pies, one pumpkin, one apple and one mincemeat, said coolly, "I went to bed at 12:30 this morning after spending all last night making pie dough, cutting up apples and mixing up the pumpkin custard and mincemeat, plus actually baking the pies.

"I really didn't feel like getting up at 5:00 a.m. to make yeast dough for the rolls on top of all that."

"But it's Thanksgiving," Livvie whined.

"Oh for chrissakes," Sally Ann snapped, "if you wanted homemade rolls so badly why didn't you make them yourself."

"Well, God, you're crabby," Olivia said. "Have you got PMS?"

No, I've got FFI, Fitzpatrick Family Insanity, Sally Ann thought wearily. "Gee, Livvie," she said sarcastically, "the fact that I'm unemployed hasn't affected my mood at all."

"Well it's your own fault you don't have a job," Livvie said snottily. "Like, you're the one who just walked away from a prestigious position with a good company. I mean, it's your own damn fault you're having to leech off Joe right now."

It's against the law to strangle one's sister, it's against the law to choke one's sister to death, Sally Ann repeated to herself as she walked away from Olivia without replying. She realized that her traditional Klonopin and carbohydrates remedy for getting through the holidays was still going to be useful. She patted her pockets, where she had stashed several of the tranquilizers, and went into the kitchen to eat some of the powdered-sugar covered walnut shortbread cookies she had also baked the night before.

Uh oh, Sally Ann thought when she saw that her mother was mixing up a blender full of margaritas. I bet I'll end up doing all the finishing touches on the dinner. She wondered briefly why she just didn't let the potatoes go unmashed and the gravy unmade while the green beans scorched in the pan, but knew that she couldn't do it. She sighed and put on an apron to cover her cashmere sweater and silk slacks.

"My but that sweater looks soft," Evelyn Fitzpatrick said. "What is it, angora?"

"Cashmere."

"Cashmere? But that's so expensive. What would your father have said?"

"He'd have been appalled and tried to make me feel like I'd committed a mortal sin by buying myself something nice. Then he'd have asked why I wasn't satisfied with a nylon sweater from Wal-Mart, and said that he thought he'd done a better job of raising me than that. Then to top it off he'd have tried to make all of us feel bad for having a nice meal 'when there are so many truly underprivileged people in this country,'" Sally Ann said sourly.

"Well, that was just your father's way, dear," Sally Ann's mother said. "He didn't really mean anything by it."

"Of course he did," Sally Ann said with an edge in her voice. "He wanted to make sure that all of us were just as miserable and guilt-ridden as he was."

"Don't speak badly about your father. He tried so hard to be a good man."

"Well his efforts were in inverse relation to the outcome."

"You know he meant well, Sally Ann."

"No I don't know that. I used to think so but I don't anymore. I mean, look at this house, Mom. It's only since he died that you've been able to get a color TV and a new stove and some nice furniture. Jesus, he wouldn't even give you enough money to buy food for the family. Dad never let you or us have anything we wanted. It's only since Dad died and you met Al that you've gotten the confidence to do some things for yourself.

"I mean," Sally Ann continued, "the material things are only symbols, Mom. Dad couldn't give to us emotionally either. I don't understand why you keep on defending him."

"You know your father loved you, Sally."

"He had a damned peculiar way of showing it. After I'd gotten out of law school and was holding down good jobs, Dad used to look at me and sigh, 'I always wanted my girls to be educated Christian ladies,' so I'd know how far below his standards I fell."

"Well, your father was very rigid and old-fashioned. He never could get used to the way you girls swear and wear short skirts and don't go to church."

"So what if I say 'shit' when I'm mad? It's not like I ever hung around bars picking up sailors. Just once . . . just once couldn't he have said he was proud of me?"

"Didn't you have any compassion at all for your dad?" Evelyn Fitzpatrick asked her daughter sadly. "He was so sick and so unhappy."

"I ate myself up with sadness for him while he was alive," Sally Ann snapped. "But he used me up—I gave everything I had to give and then burned up all my reserves on top of that. Now that he's dead there's nothing left." She thought about her father's last trip to the hospital, when she had held his hand in the ambulance as he wept, knowing that he'd never see his home again. She remembered how she had sobbed helplessly the next day after he'd died, gripping the bars of the hospital gurney on which her father's shrunken body lay alone in an empty room. She had been bent double from the anguish she felt over her father's sad, wasted life and the fact that she had never been able to make things right for him or for her mother.

Her mother didn't answer. Instead she stood staring at the pitcher of margaritas with the wounded, pathetic look on her face that always reduced Sally Ann to a psychic lump of quivering guilt. "Your father and I tried to do our best by you girls," she finally said with a catch in her voice.

Oh, fuck, now I've made her cry, Sally Ann thought frantically. Won't I ever learn that there's absolutely no point in trying to talk to any member of my family about anything?

She walked over to the counter and patted her mother's shoulder. "I'm sorry, Mom. I guess I'm just on edge because of what happened with my job. Why don't you pass out the drinks and I'll finish up the dinner."

Evelyn Fitzpatrick poured the foamy green margaritas from the blender container into a crystal pitcher Sally Ann had given her for Christmas one year. "Do you want a taste, dear?"

"No thanks."

"Since you brought it up, I just want to say that I'm glad you quit your job. I hated your having to work for that awful man. I always wanted to call him up and tell him to quit being so mean to my little girl."

"Oh, Mom. I'm glad I quit, too. Now I just need to figure out a way to earn some money."

"Why don't you let Joe take care of you for a while? He earns a good living. I've never understood why you girls are all so set on making your own way. When I got married women expected their husbands to support them."

We didn't want to end up like you and your lady friends, Sally Ann thought. She didn't say anything, partly because she didn't know if her mother remembered getting slapped around by Sally's father when she was in the depths of her depressions. Sally Ann often thought that the numbing effects of heavy medication and hundreds of shock treatments had blitzed whatever of her mother's long-term memory cells that hadn't been destroyed by her depressive illness itself.

Evelyn Fitzpatrick put the crystal pitcher of frozen margaritas on a tray with four long-stemmed glasses. "I guess Joe won't be having any, will he?" she asked.

"No. I'll get him a Coke when he wants it."

"All right, dear." Sally Ann's mother walked from the kitchen into the living room where Al, Joe and Livvie's husband Stan were playing computer games on Al's PC. "Who wants a margarita?" Sally Ann heard her mother ask.

Hurrying around the kitchen, Sally Ann did all the last-minute work needed to put a big holiday meal on the table while her relatives drank and played computer games. She didn't really mind doing everything since being in her mother's house made her so jumpy she couldn't sit still.

During the last miserable years of Francis Fitzpatrick's prolonged dying and the months following his death, Sally Ann had felt as though a visible cloud of misery hung over the small rowhouse. She had gotten physically ill from the tension every time she went there but doggedly kept on doing what she thought was her duty.

Thanks to Al's genial presence and her mother's late-found happiness, the house was no longer permeated with anger and fear and depression. But Sally Ann's memories remained; she often wished that her mother would sell the house and get a fresh start with Al in a neutral place.

"Need any help?" Joe walked into the kitchen, then opened the refrigerator looking for soft drinks.

"You could take the Waldorf salad out of the fridge and put it on the dining room table."

"I'm sorry, miss, but we're all out of waldorfs today," Joe said in his best John Cleese voice.

"I knew you'd say that." Sally Ann looked affectionately at her husband. "Hey, quit eating the walnuts out of the salad."

"Nag, nag, nag." Joe smiled at his wife.

"Now I need you to help me get the turkey out of the oven."

Together Sally and Joe wrestled the 20-pound turkey out of the roasting pan and onto the platter. Sally Ann raced around the kitchen, dishing up the dressing, gravy, fresh cranberry relish, mashed potatoes, and other vegetables into serving bowls that Joe placed on the dining table. She put the warmed-up, although not homemade, rolls into the bread server. "What am I forgetting?" she asked Joe.

"Is this for today's dinner?" Joe said, pulling out a glass relish tray loaded with olives, vegetable sticks and marinated cheese cubes from the refrigerator.

"That's what I was forgetting. Okay, I think that's it." Sally Ann walked into the living room where her mother and step-father, sister and brother-in-law were mellowed out on margaritas. "Come on, people, dinner's on the table," she said. "Al, if you could carve the turkey, and Olivia, if you'd pour the wine, we can eat."

An hour later, after everyone had eaten himself into a state of torpor and the table had been cleared, Evelyn Fitzpatrick asked, "Who wants pie and coffee?"

"I want a tiny slice of each kind of pie," Livvie Ann answered. "And please put a little bit of ice cream on the apple and a spoonful of whipped cream on the pumpkin."

"Glad you have such a dainty appetite," Stan sarcastically told his wife. Livvie glared at him.

Before the two of them could start another round of their endless bickering, Sally Ann, who was looking out the front window, said "Uh oh. Jehovah's Witnesses alert."

"On a holiday?" everyone else chorused.

"They don't celebrate holidays," Joe said. "These folks probably figured they'd have a better chance of catching everyone at home if they cruised the neighborhood on Thanksgiving afternoon." He looked out the window and watched the neatly-dressed trio, two women and a man, start up the sidewalk to the Fitzpatrick house.

The doorbell rang. "Should we just ignore it?" Olivia asked hopefully.

"No," Al said. "They'll stand out there for fifteen minutes ringing the bell and pounding on the door before they'll go away." He went to answer the door, then came back a minute later. "Sally, if you'll cut three slices of pie and put them on paper plates for the Witnesses, they said they'll go away."

"A small price to pay." Sally Ann hurried into the kitchen to get the paper plates and plastic forks.

After Al had delivered the pie and refused copies of 'The Watchtower," he returned to the dining table, smiling broadly. "I think they're eating Thanksgiving dinner in stages by going door to door. Everyone's bribing them to go away."

"I guess that's one way to get a nice Thanksgiving dinner without having to admit you're celebrating a holiday," Stan said. "What a bunch of weirdos."

The telephone rang. Speaking of weirdos, Sally Ann thought, who will this be—Laurie or Claire?

"Well, Laurie, dear, how nice to hear from you," Sally Ann heard her mother saying into the telephone.

Al looked sour. "She must be broke again—that's the only time she calls your mother."

"Well, she never calls me," Sally Ann said.

"Small loss," Joe said quietly. Al laughed.

"Girls, it's your sister Laurie Ann. Who wants to talk to her first?" Sally's mother came into the room carrying a portable phone.

"I do." Olivia jumped up and took the handset from her mother. She was soon talking animatedly, telling Laurie about the latest acquisition her department at the Museum of Art had gotten for its permanent collection. After a lengthy discussion of seventeenth-century Dutch genre paintings with her favorite sister, Livvie reluctantly gave the phone to Sally Ann. "Here. Laurie wants to say hi."

"Hi, Laurie," Sally Ann said with false cheerfulness.

"Oh Sally," her sister gushed, "it's been so long. I just had to talk to you and catch up with what's going on in your life." She then descended into one of her famous Laurie monologues, during which, for 20 minutes, Sally Ann's only words were 'oh, really' and 'uh huh.'

"And then Grete and I went to a Goddess healing ceremony yesterday to begin our holiday," Laurie burbled on after telling Sally Ann all about her new female lover, who was originally from Amsterdam (the sixth 'greatest love of her life' after her five former husbands if Sally Ann hadn't lost count), their art gallery in Santa Fe, the superiority of same-sex relationships, Grete's spirituality, and so on and so on.

"Oh Sally," Laurie said breathlessly, "that ceremony was so meaningful. It took place at dawn and culminated as the sun rose. All of us were so moved we were in tears, just absolutely overwhelmed by the peace and harmony."

Sally Ann mentally pictured the aging Boomer women in their retro-hippie earth mother muumuus and meaningful, handcrafted, albeit quite ugly, jewelry.

"I just felt so spiritual, so connected with all of womankind, so at one with the Goddess who's within each of us," Laurie continued. "Grete and I were both overwhelmed," she repeated, "just bursting with emotion."

Sally Ann heroically refrained from making an inappropriate comment about stopping the flood of feelings with a finger in the Dutch dyke.

"Well, that's enough about me. What's going on in your life?" Laurie finally asked her sister.

"I quit my job," Sally Ann answered.

"Well, good for you," Laurie said. "Listen, I'd love to chat with you about it, but my goodness we've been talking for ages and my phone bill is going to be astronomical. You'll have to tell me everything next time we talk. Say hi to Joe for me. Take care. Bye."

The phone clicked and the connection was broken.

Unbelievable, Sally Ann thought. She looked over at Joe who was smiling sympathetically at her. "And happy Thanksgiving to you, too, Laurie Ann," Sally said into the air. She smiled cynically back at her husband.

By then it was late afternoon and the brief November day was ending. Al built a fire in the fireplace. Sally Ann sat on the floor staring at the flickering orange and yellow flames, mesmerized by their movement and light, while Livvie, Stan and her mother played Scrabble and Joe read one of Al's computer magazines. Al, who had once been a professional musician, sat at the battered old upright piano, skillfully playing old swing tunes from the 1940s.

Everyone had finally relaxed and there was a warm, family feeling in the room. Sally Ann wondered wistfully what it would be like to have relatives who made her feel close and connected all the time.

Catholics, Crazies and Lawyers

Two weeks to the day after Christmas, Louise and Sally Ann celebrated the joint Sally-Elvis birthday by going shopping in Center City, then having coffee and dessert at the Borders bookstore on Walnut Street.

"Here's to the King," Louise lifted her cup of double latte in a mock toast, "and to my friend Sally Ann."

"To Elvis and me." Sally Ann raised her cup of steaming Darjeeling. "Let's honor Mr. Presley by indulging in soon-to-be regulated substances."

"What do you mean?"

138 · N. E. JULIAN

"I heard on the news that there are now twelve-step groups for coffee drinkers. Being a recovering caffeine addict is a newly fashionable disorder."

"Good grief," Louise said in disgust. "Aren't any pleasures going to be left to us?"

"Nope. Pretty soon suburbanites will be furtively selling little plastic bags of Kona Blend from the backs of their Range Rovers."

"Then I guess I'll be breaking the law," Louise said. "I can't live without my coffee. Will you come and visit me in jail, Sally?"

"You bet. Besides, my mother will probably be in the cell next to yours. She'll have been picked up on tobacco charges."

"First the smokers, then the coffee-drinkers, who'll be next?"

"The chocoholics and tea-drinkers. I guess I'd better start stockpiling tea bags and chocolate chips."

"Everything to excess, that's what I always say." Louise took a dainty bite of her double-fudge layer cake with mocha frosting, then said, "After the new Prohibition gets imposed, what will there be left to do?"

"Eat lentil casseroles and sit around resoling our Birkenstocks, I guess."

"Ugh." Louise slowly licked a big dollop of whipped cream from her spoon. "How was your Christmas?"

"Pretty bad. We went to my in-laws' house for Christmas dinner since we had Thanksgiving with my side of the family." Sally Ann drank some tea. "I'll tell you, Louise, if there were an Olympic competition for petty nastiness, Joe's parents would be gold medalists. I've never figured out how the two of them produced him."

"Y'all still aren't getting along, I take it?"

"The state of open warfare that's existed between us since the day Joe first introduced us sixteen years ago had frozen into armed neutrality on both sides. They wouldn't come out and openly admit they can't stand me, and for Joe's sake I tried to be polite, but then my mother-in-law decided to ratchet up the hostilities on Christmas day."

"What did she do?"

"She invited us to Christmas dinner, then ate without us."

"What?"

"My dear mother-in-law told us that dinner was at two p.m., we showed up at 1:30, and found out that Joe's parents and all his other relatives were just finishing up dessert."

KEY WEST DREAMS · 139

Louise sucked in her breath. "Are you sure there wasn't a mix-up about the time?"

"It wasn't a mix-up, it was a set-up. She actually called us at noon, 'just to confirm that we'd be there by two.' I realized when we got to my in-laws' house that she must have phoned right before calling everyone to the table."

"What did you do?"

"I was speechless. I stood by the dining room table and just stared at Joe's mother while his aunts and uncles looked embarrassed. Then she put on the perky high-school girl routine she uses when she's being really obnoxious and said she'd go into the kitchen and dish up our dinners 'because she'd saved the best for us.'"

"I'd have told her where she could stick her damn leftovers," Louise said.

"I couldn't eat. I wanted to walk out, but for Joe's sake I didn't."

"What did Joe do?"

"Nothing. He's a man and she's his mother."

"Joe's not an only child, is he?"

"No, he has a younger sister. But he's the first-born and only son, and his parents have seen me as competition for their baby boy's affection from day one." Sally Ann slowly chewed a bite of her Linzer torte, savoring the buttery, nutty shortbread crust and red-raspberry preserve topping.

"I'll give you the only advice I ever voluntarily offer people, Louise—if you get married, live at least 600 miles from both sets of parents. Your life will be much easier ... Also, don't marry an only child or an only son—his mother will hate you for the rest of her life, no matter what you do."

"Well, on that note, I have to tell you that when I went back to Texas for Christmas one of my cousins introduced me to a guy who might have real possibilities."

"Love is on the horizon?"

"I don't know about love ... but definitely serious like."

"So tell me about him."

"He's a teacher in the music department at a private prep school, plays sax in a jazz band, likes classical music, and isn't gay or bi—... and he's decent looking."

"Any drawbacks?

"Divorced, two children who live with their mother . . . plus, he lives in Denton and I'm here, so we'll have to see how things shape up. But for now they're looking good."

"Now I know why you're carbo-loading," Sally Ann said. "You're in sex-withdrawal."

"Yep." Louise licked more whipped cream from her spoon.

"Well, congratulations. I hope things work out. How did the rest of your visit go?"

"Oh, fine. I got to see all my aunts and uncles and cousins. We had us a big old party that lasted from Christmas Eve to New Year's."

"How's your dad doing?"

"Oh, fine . . . but my stepmother hates me as much as ever. I must have sorely peeved that woman in a former life, and I'm paying for it now."

"Who knows," Sally Ann said. "Maybe she's just a bitch."

"I do love talking to you, Sally," Louise said, smiling at her friend. The two women sat quietly for a few minutes, eating their pastries and savoring the relaxed, comfortable moment.

Two young voices drifted into the coffee bar from the bookcases that came to the edge of the bar's railings.

"I just don't get it," a twenty-something female voice said. "Who is this Doc Johnson person?"

"Shh," an embarrassed young male voice replied. "Not so loud."

"But who is he?"

"He's not a person. 'Doc Johnson' is the name of a line of sex toys. You know, it's a take-off on slang for a guy's . . . you know."

"I don't get it." The two voices faded into murmurs.

"Oh for God's sake," Sally Ann said to Louise. "They're in the Art section—why doesn't he draw her a picture?"

Louise snickered. "How could anyone be that dense?"

"Makes a person wonder about today's youth, doesn't it?" Looking at the unkempt young people sitting at the rest of the coffee bar's tables, Sally Ann added, "Sometimes I feel like a dinosaur."

Louise said disparagingly, "Why do these kids think that being intelligent precludes good grooming?"

"They're being non-conformist by dressing and thinking alike. Besides, remember last summer when all the preppie girls were wearing their mothers' old Lilly Pulitzer shifts and the boys had the retro-50s look: chinos and crewcuts. I'm not sure which is worse—grungy pseudo-intellectuals or bland neo-suburbanites.

"So how are you going to be a proto-slacker without dressing like one?" Louise asked.

"I've had to re-think my goals," Sally Ann answered. "I'm still not interested in doing much besides lying on the couch and reading, but I think I've outgrown sitting around and having endless meaningful conversations with terminally serious people."

She added, "Maybe I'm a post-yuppie or a burned-out Boomer. I guess I have until my unemployment benefits run out to decide."

A young man sitting at the next table interjected himself into the conversation. "Why worry about meaningless labels?" he asked earnestly, running his fingers through his straight, shoulder-length brown hair, then taking an affected puff on his pipe. "The pervading nihilistic mood makes all categories useless."

"I'll tell you, Maynard," Louise said as she gathered up her purse and packages, "eating and screwing, that's what it all comes down to."

Sally Ann picked up her purse and stood up.

"Maynard?" the young slacker asked, bewildered. "That's not my name."

"Don't you ever watch the 'Dobie Gillis' reruns on cable TV?" Louise said.

"I don't watch television," he said pompously.

"Why doesn't that surprise me?" Louise replied.

Sally Ann looked at the boy and said gently, "It's none of my business but you won't lose any brain cells if you lighten up and laugh every now and then." She immediately wondered if she had been presumptuous. She remembered how, as a teenager and young woman, she had become so angry when, overwhelmed by her attempts to carry the burden of her family's troubles, well-meaning older people had patronizingly assumed she couldn't have any problems because she was young and pretty. Taking a closer look at the boy, she decided his air of self-conscious angst was too affected to come from real pain.

"Women," the kid said contemptuously. "Even the ones like you who seem intelligent ultimately transcend logic."

"'Woman having so much power by nature, the law rightly gives her none,'" Sally Ann said.

"Huh?" the kid asked blankly.

"That's a paraphrase of a quote from the English jurist Blackstone's commentary on eighteenth-century matrimonial law."

"How do you know that?" he asked suspiciously.

"Because I went to law school, where my ability to transcend logic served me well when I learned about our legal system."

The young man's face turned red above his scraggly beard and he looked helplessly around the coffee bar.

Sally Ann reached for her shopping bag. "I'll leave you with one final thought."

"What's that?" he asked weakly.

"Jimmy Buffett forever."

Sally Ann and Louise smiled and walked out of the coffee bar. "I bet he hasn't gotten laid recently," Louise said, once they were out of the boy's earshot.

"I wouldn't be that age again for anything," Sally Ann said with a shudder. "Watching these clueless kids makes me realize all over again how awful it is to be young."

"You've got that right."

"People used to tell me that my high school and college years were going to be the best part of my life. All I could think at the time was, if this is the best then I'm jumping off a bridge right now because I don't want to live through the worst."

"So, do you have any idea what you're going to do now that you've quit your job—don't answer if I'm getting too personal," Louise asked as she and Sally Ann browsed through the bookstore's current fiction display.

"I ran an ad in the local legal newspaper saying I'm available to do *per diem* work for other lawyers," Sally Ann answered. "You know, stuff like doing their research, writing their briefs. A guy from my law school class who has his own law practice called me last week and asked me to do several projects for him."

She picked up the latest Kinky Friedman mystery, saying, "I kind of enjoy legal writing. I can analyze legal issues without actually having to deal with other lawyers since my name won't be on the briefs."

"Oh, Kinky Friedman," Louise said with enthusiasm. "The original Jewish Texan country-western singer/mystery writer."

"The original? Don't you mean the only?" Sally Ann asked.

"Why don't you use your time off to write a novel?" Louise asked.

"About what?" Sally Ann answered. "My life's experience is limited to dealing with Catholics, crazies and lawyers . . . most of whom fall into more than one category."

"There has to be a story in there somewhere."

"Well, I must admit that one of my English teachers at St. Jude the Obscure Preparatory Academy told me I should be a writer when I grew up. But then I fell from her favor when I wrote a book report on *Atlas Shrugged* in which I made favorable references to Ayn Rand's views on selfishness and objectivism."

"How old were you—I didn't know that Ayn Rand is taught in high school."

"She wasn't, at least not in freshman English when I was fourteen," Sally Ann said. "Everyone in my class had been told to write a report on any book we thought was a classic; there was no list of approved titles so I chose *Atlas Shrugged* which I was already reading at the time."

"So what happened?" Louise asked.

"Oh, there was a huge flap. The nun wrote a note to my parents telling them I was seriously lacking in Catholic values, my father got hysterical and said he wasn't going to waste his money educating an atheist daughter, blah, blah, blah, then he threatened to send me to a public high school."

"So why didn't you go?" Louise asked. "As much as you hated the nuns that would have been your chance to get away from them."

"I should have left. But at the time I thought it was a point of honor not to let my dad push me around, so I ended up wasting three more years at that place . . . Besides, my parents' house is in the Philadelphia school district, and you know how bad the Philly schools are. At least at St. Jude's everyone could read."

"You Catholics certainly have interesting childhoods."

"Ex-Catholic, in my case. And because of the Catholic school system, large numbers of therapists in this country have good incomes and long-term clienteles."

"So how did Joe turn out to be so normal?"

"Because he's a Protestant," Sally Ann said, laughing. "I'd never marry a Catholic man. Most of them are so screwed up by the church's teachings about sex as sin and women as the gateway to hell that they go to one of two extremes. Either they're almost eunuchs from guilt or they try to pork every female in sight as a way of proving their religion isn't strangling them.

"To change the subject completely," Sally Ann added, "I'm going to pay for this Kinky Friedman book before I get picked up for shoplifting."

"Okay. I'll be looking at greeting cards while you're in line," Louise said.

After Sally Ann had gotten through the cashier's line, she walked over to Louise who was holding a card and laughing. "You've got to see this, Sally."

Sally Ann looked at the birthday card, the front of which had a photo of a very pretty blonde girl under a caption reading, 'Remember, on your latest birthday . . .' while on the inside it said ' . . . she's young enough to be your daughter.'

"That's cold," she said. "This reminds me of the card I was going to send one of my sisters on her last birthday. The front read, 'Love can fade, diamonds may crack . . .' then the inside said 'but cellulite is forever.'"

Louise laughed. "That's awful. Where on earth did you find a card that mean?"

"I made it myself. But then Joe talked me out of sending it. He thinks that people should never burn their bridges. I told him that first there have to be bridges to burn . . . but then I decided it would be better to put the card in with my file of unsent family letters."

"Is that where your 'Merry Christmas and Screw You, Bitch' cards went last year?"

"Yeah. Joe persuaded me not to send them to my sisters. I didn't tell him that I'd set aside one for his mother, too."

The two women left Borders, pushing through the heavy glass revolving door into the cold grey of a late winter afternoon. Sally Ann gave a dollar to a homeless man who was begging in the shelter of the store's doorway.

"You're just enabling him to stay on the street," Louise said disapprovingly. "He should be in a shelter or a drug treatment program."

"That's the conventional wisdom," Sally Ann said, "but to me not giving money to someone who's homeless and hungry makes about as much sense as telling a drowning person he should have learned to swim.

"Besides," she added, "that man could be you or me or any person who's in the wrong place under the wrong circumstances. Anybody can get broken by life."

Louise didn't reply although she glanced back at the ragged, hollow-eyed man with a trace of compassion.

The two women walked briskly down Walnut Street, burrowing inside their coats and clutching their packages but still looking into the brightly-lit shop windows.

"Well, Louise," Sally Ann said, "we've shopped until we dropped, eaten and drunk things that are bad for us, bought books, and talked ourselves out. Think it's time to go home?"

"I think so," Louise answered. "Happy birthday, Elvis, wherever you are. We've had a good time today in your memory. And happy birthday to you, Sally."

Sally Ann and her friend raced to Louise's car which was parked in an open lot a few blocks away. They threw their packages and bags into the back seat of the ancient Cadillac Louise's father had given her years ago when he bought himself a new one, then hurriedly settled themselves into the deep front seats. "Turn on the heat, please," Sally Ann said, her teeth chattering.

They sat huddled in their coats as the old car's heater reluctantly warmed up.

"You know, I bet it's about 80 degrees and sunny in Key West," Sally Ann said. "I've got an idea. Why don't we drive to our houses, pick up Othello and Joe and head south."

"Don't tempt me," Louise said as she drove her car out of the lot. "But we'd have to take a detour to Texas so I could get my sax player."

The two women happily plotted their escape from winter, bills and responsibility as Louise drove home through a fine blanket of snow and sleet which had just begun to fall.

Chapter Nine

No Neurotic Need To Be Productive

If I Had a Lawyer For a Client, I'd Hang Myself

For many attorneys, the ultimate refuge, even more so than their favorite bar, is the county legal association's law library which is usually maintained in the county courthouse or in a building nearby. Under the guise of researching sources not available in their firms' libraries, the lawyers find peace and quiet away from their supervising attorneys, their secretaries and their clients yet still manage to rack up billable hours.

At one time lawyers also came to the library to get away from their telephones' constant interruptions. Sally Ann had noticed that lately, however, in addition to their pocket dictating equipment, a number of the more gung-ho weenies were bringing their cell phones with them to the Philadelphia Bar Association's Jenkins Memorial Law Library.

Sally Ann looked with irritation at one wimpy, suspendered young man with slicked-back hair as he whispered self-importantly into his phone while sitting at one of the tables in the library's Pennsylvania section. She thought that Jenkins should make everyone check their phones at the front desk the way saloonkeepers in cowboy movies made the men leave their weapons by the front door.

She sighed and went back to the plaintiff's response to a defendant's motion for summary judgment that she was drafting for her former classmate, Jon Rabinowitz. Sally Ann had been working on the document for several days, first doing hours of legal research into the applicable law, then writing the response and supporting brief. She knew that she probably wouldn't bill Jon for at least a third of her time, since Jon was paying her on an hourly basis and she didn't want her fee to be so high he wouldn't send her any more work.

Her mind wandered. Scanning the tables and carrels in the library's crowded state section, Sally Ann looked either for people she knew or good-looking men. No one she recognized was there, but sitting at the opposite side of the table in front of hers was a quite decent-looking specimen of male attorney: mid-30s to 40, neat brown hair that wasn't slicked back, nice face, broad shoulders, well-cut suit. Since he was sitting down she couldn't tell his height but would have bet he was around six feet tall.

This day is looking up, Sally Ann thought as she discreetly eyed the man.

An attractive woman wearing a well-tailored navy suit and carrying an armload of case reporters walked past the man's table, then turned back as she recognized him. "Hi, Jack," she said quietly but with a smile. "What are you doing here?" She put her law books on the table, then sat down next to the man.

"Hi, Erica," Jack said. "I'm escaping from the office for a while."

"Same here," Erica said ruefully. "Everything is particularly crazy at work today. So, what's new with you?"

Jack sighed and drummed his fingers on the table's edge. "My firm's agreed to do defense work for one of the professional liability insurers. So I'm defending another lawyer in a legal malpractice case . . . and he's making me crazy. He calls me at least four times a day, second-guesses everything I do, and is completely illogical and intransigent—not to mention rude, abrasive and arrogant.

"I've come close to punching out that jerk several times, so now I don't meet with him face-to-face if I can avoid it. That's why he telephones so much. I'd gotten three calls this morning before 10:30, so I said screw it and came to the library."

"Oh, my God," Erica groaned. "That's so awful—a lawyer for a client. I think I'd hang myself before I'd represent another attorney."

"Yeah, well, I may end up strangling him before this case is over."

"Shh!" a voice coming from one of the carrels admonished fiercely. Looking guilty, the two lawyers lowered their voices and continued murmuring to each other.

Sally Ann smiled and went back to work, crafting well-reasoned rebuttals that refuted, point by point, each contention raised in the defendant's motion for summary judgment. She was writing her brief the old-fashioned way, with a fountain pen on a legal pad, since she didn't have a laptop computer.

Unlike the lawyer who had drafted the defendant's motion, Sally Ann wasn't cobbling together sections of previously-written documents pulled from a computer's memory. She was, instead, putting together an original, well thought out document tailored specifically to the facts of Jon's client's case.

This *per diem* work isn't so bad, she thought. I get the file from Jon, he tells me what he needs, and I do it. I make my own hours, there's no one around to bother me, and I don't have to hassle with the clients or opposing counsel.

God, maybe I should think about trying to build up a network of four or five solo practitioners who'd do like Jon and send me their big writing projects. I might never have to get a real job again. The thought of never having to work for another lawyer, or of having any boss but herself, was so elating that Sally Ann got dizzy.

In the weeks since she had quit her job, Sally Ann had been on a number of interviews for temporary or part-time legal positions. Each had convinced her that a large percentage, perhaps the majority, of practicing attorneys had serious personality problems.

There had been the judge who grilled her about why she didn't have children; the two women lawyers who took her to lunch at a Main Line country club and spent the meal ripping apart most of their society acquaintances, then speculating about whether Kip or Tibby would get the club membership in their divorce settlement; the tax lawyer who had made tasteless jokes about hemorrhoids and the medication Anusol (which he continually mispronounced as 'anus-oil') while interviewing her. Sally Ann's most recent encounter had been with two personal injury ambulance chasers who needed a part-time attorney to help them tackle the mountain of legal papers their litigation practice generated.

At the outset of their first, and only, meeting, Sally Ann had immediately noticed that the nominal senior partner, a man with a soft face, weak mouth and limp handshake, totally deferred to his junior partner, a coarsely attractive man who talked continually and disjointedly about himself, his achievements, and his recent divorce during her alleged interview.

"My ex-wife loves to go to her lawyer's office, dressed up and carrying a briefcase and pretending she's somebody . . . but I'm fighting her every step of the way," he told Sally Ann, his voice vindictive. "She's never getting my kids. *I'm* the one who's taken care of them at every step of the way since we split up. Hell, *I'm* even the person who showed my girls what to do when they started to menstruate."

I just bet your kids would love your telling that particular piece of news to a complete stranger, Sally Ann had thought. She was saved from having to reply by the man's switching in mid-sentence to telling her what an honor it would be for her to get to work for an attorney having his professional standing. Sally had only smiled, thinking that she'd never heard of the lawyer or his partner until she saw their ad in the legal newspaper.

When the two men showed her around their converted townhouse on the edge of Philadelphia's Old City historic district, she saw a bullet-riddled human silhouette target hanging on the back wall of one office next to the attorney's framed degrees and professional awards. Then she found pornography sitting on the bathroom radiator when she asked to use the restroom.

After first asking Sally Ann if she would be offended by 'coarse talk' in the office ("I love to talk about my prick," the junior partner had said with a leering smile), the two attorneys had offered her the position. She had turned them down and left their offices, feeling as if she needed to take a shower.

I guess I've gotten a little smarter, Sally Ann thought as she took a mental break from Jon's project. At one time I would have agreed to work for those creeps just because I need the money. Now all I've done is dedicate a poem to them.

She pulled a loose piece of lined paper from the back of her leather portfolio. On it was written a poem she had composed in response to a crack Joe made after she told him about the magazines she had seen in the two lawyers' bathroom.

> My wife divorced me/My girlfriend ran away/It's just the two of us/Little buddy, would you like to play?

> My Porsche got rear-ended/My client lied on the stand,/Seems like all I've got left/Is you and my right hand.

> My dog can't stand me,/The girls all say I'm a jerk,/If not for you, all I could screw/Is my clients at work.

> The judge cut back my contingency fee,/My tailor said I've gained weight,/You're looking better and better to me,/Little buddy, let's go on a date.

Sally Ann pulled a new piece of blank paper from her legal pad. Addressing it to Mr. Jimmy Buffett, President, Margaritaville Records, she wrote: 'Dear Mr. Buffett, I am a lawyer-turned-songwriter. Enclosed herewith is my original work, 'A One-Handed Lover's Lament,' which I am submitting to you for use by yourself or one of your label's artists.'

Crumpling up both sheets of paper, Sally tossed them into the trash can. It must be time for lunch, she thought. My mind is really starting to wander. She decided to go to the Twentieth Street Bar and Grill, to see if anything had changed in the months since she had worked in Center City.

Although she intended to return to the library, Sally Ann packed her briefcase, stuffing all her notes and the half-written draft of her brief into it. The library was posted with signs warning the lawyers not to leave their personal belongings unattended. So much for honor among thieves, she thought.

On her way out she stopped by the ladies' room. Taped to the mirror was a notice from the chief legal librarian, listing recent acts of vandalism at the library. Sally Ann smiled sardonically when she saw that first on the list was theft of current ethical rulings by the Pennsylvania attorneys' disciplinary board—some enterprising lawyer who didn't want to pay for copies had razor-bladed the pages from the book.

It was a cold, raw winter day; Sally Ann huddled into her coat, carrying her purse and briefcase in her gloved hands as she walked briskly down the street after getting off the city bus she had ridden from the law library. All she could think about was how cold she was and how much she wanted a bowl of hot soup. When she got to the restaurant's site, she ended up walking past it. The Twentieth Street Bar's familiar sign and awning were gone.

Sally Ann stood outside the restaurant, looking in disbelief at its new sign which read 'Montego Bay.' She was too cold to stand gawking on the street so she walked into the building. The restaurant's former, slightly shabby, wood floor and wooden tables ambience was gone. The floor was painted in a bright yellow and red checkerboard, the walls were bright green, and stuffed parrots in wire rings hung from the ceiling. Slightly out of tune steel drum music played over the sound system.

She continued scanning the restaurant, which was almost empty even though it was the peak business lunchtime. A black server walked toward her; she saw that the man was Aaron although at first she didn't recognize him since he was dressed in linen slacks and a loud Hawaiian shirt.

"Well, this makes my day," Aaron said, a delighted smile on his face. "Where have you been, girl?"

"I quit my job last fall," Sally Ann answered. "It's a long story. What's happened here, Aaron?"

Aaron looked disconsolately around the patron-free restaurant. "Right before Christmas we had to close because of water damage from a broken pipe. The owner decided the restaurant had gotten boring and banal, so since we were closed anyway, he redecorated, changed the name and changed the menu."

"Um . . . how's business?" Sally Ann asked politely.

"You can see for yourself," Aaron said, waving toward the empty front dining room. "There's almost no one in the back, either . . . Do you want your old table by the window?"

152 · N. E. JULIAN

"Please."

When she was seated, Sally Ann took another look at the restaurant's walls. She saw that the large painted party scene which had always hung on the Twentieth Street's right front wall was gone.

"What happened to the painting, Aaron?" she asked.

"Everyone wants to know that. The owner decided the picture was as banal as everything else, so he took it home and stuck it in his basement."

"Jeez," Sally Ann said. "What a waste . . . So, what's the soup today?"

"Black bean and coconut," Aaron said with a grimace. "We've got Caribbean cuisine now. Do you want to see the menu?"

"I guess," Sally Ann said dubiously.

Ten minutes later she was staring even more dubiously at a plate of what the menu called conch fritters. She had never eaten them before and had no idea how the dish was supposed to taste. But once she ate her first mouthful of the greasy fried batter wrapped around stringy shreds of tough grey shellfish meat, she knew that the soggy lumps sitting on her plate couldn't be state of the art.

Sally Ann forced herself to swallow what was in her mouth instead of discreetly spitting it into her napkin. She ate a buttered roll and finished drinking her tea, then asked Aaron for the check.

"Do you want me to see if the manager will take this off your ticket?" Aaron asked as he picked up the plate of uneaten fritters.

"No, don't bother." Sally Ann handed Aaron enough money to cover the bill plus a generous tip. "It's been good to see you again, Aaron," she said as she stood and put on her coat.

"It's been good to see you too, Sally," Aaron said. "Since the changeover we've lost all our old client base." He looked around the restaurant and then lowered his voice. "Most of the new people don't come back after their first time here."

I wonder why, Sally Ann thought sarcastically, feeling her one bite of conch fritter sitting heavily and greasily in her stomach. She smiled sympathetically at Aaron and patted his arm. "I've got to get back to the law library. You take care of yourself, okay?"

"I don't have any choice," Aaron answered. "Don't you go doing anything I wouldn't do."

"Since we both like guys, that's unlikely."

Aaron laughed and handed Sally her briefcase. "Stop in and say hi if you're in the neighborhood—I won't expect you to eat any of the new chef's food."

"I'll do that." Sally Ann walked to the front door then turned and waved to Aaron, who was still standing by her table. She went outside and felt the cold, raw dampness cutting through her. Standing on the street corner, she shivered and waited for the bus that would take her back to the law library.

He Ain't Heavy, He's My Bubba

Sally Ann lay in bed beside Joe who was engulfed in the happy dreamless sleep of a sexually-satisfied male. Sally was equally satisfied but not sleepy so she lay on her back, her head elevated on her bunched-up pillow, listening to Bubba snore while her mind wandered contentedly.

The three of them were in a hotel room in San Francisco. Joe had asked Sally Ann to accompany him on a business trip since he was tired of traveling by himself. Sally, who was even more tired of staying home alone, had agreed to go but only if she could bring Bubba.

"He's getting too old to board, Joe," she had said stubbornly as her husband tried to talk her out of taking their dog on a cross-country trip. "Besides, no one at the vet's will scratch his ears and hum 'Let Me Call You Sweetheart' to him like I do."

"God I hope not," Joe had said with derision, looking affectionately at his wife who was sitting on the floor by the couch, rubbing their fat old terrier's curly white stomach as his little toes curled blissfully.

"Besides," Sally Ann had added, "Bubba sleeps most of the time these days. He's a wreck if he doesn't get his 20 hours a day. So he'll spend his time sleeping in the hotel room."

"Oh, all right," Joe had given in with good grace. "Bring your baby if you have to."

They had been in San Francisco for three days. Each morning Sally Ann got up early and ordered room-service breakfasts while Joe walked Bubba. The two of them usually got back around the time the food was delivered. After Sally and Joe ate and Bubba begged successfully, Sally Ann would kiss Joe goodbye as he left for work.

She would go to the hotel's spa and exercise, then come back to the room and shower. When the maid came, she took Bubba for another stroll while the room was cleaned. She would leave for lunch and an afternoon exploring on her own as Bubba slept, curled up in a nest of pillows on the bed. To make him feel at home, she'd put a Buffett tape on and set it to continually replay until she returned. No matter how restless Bubba was, the sound of the singer's familiar twangy baritone always soothed him. Sally Ann had noticed that her dog was particularly fond of the 'Last Mango in Paris' cassette, with 'Songs You Know by Heart: Jimmy Buffett's Greatest Hit(s)' coming in a close second.

Lying in bed, contentedly pressed against Joe's solid warmth, Sally thought that only a few months ago she would have been embarrassed to be the tag-along wife on her husband's business trip. When she first quit her job, along with the relief and anxiety had come her irrational belief that anyone looking at her knew she was unemployed. She would reluctantly go out into public, feeling that she was emanating 'jobless loser' rays and that everyone was staring at her. It had surprised her to find out that, like Karen Brennan, she felt diminished without paid employment.

Now Sally Ann didn't care. For the first time in her life, she was slowly beginning to relax; it was such a wonderful feeling that most of the time she thought that inner peace was well worth the price of her vanished career.

Even as a child Sally Ann had been tense and unhappy. She had absorbed the anger and anxiety in her parents' relationship, while the repressive parochial schools she attended had only added to the dull greyness in which she lived. Over everything had hung the unspoken pall of her mother's recurring depressions and her father's complete inability to cope.

Sally Ann's sole refuge had been herself. As the years passed she turned from a confident, outgoing small child into one who was too withdrawn to make friends. The only person in her family who appeared to value her was her mother, and then only when she wasn't depressed. She learned from an early age to keep her problems to herself. "Don't bother your mother," Francis Fitzpatrick always told his daughters, "you'll make her get sick again."

Photographs from Sally's childhood showed a thin, owlish child wearing glasses and an almost permanent scowl. She read constantly to escape the reality of her life and her isolation within her family and at school, where her intellect cut her off from the children of the knee-jerk Catholics who were packed into the bulging parish classrooms of the baby boom years.

She thought her life had improved when she met Joe. His warmth and kindness were like sunshine that dissipated the cold fog of sadness that surrounded her. Gradually she had gotten some of her self-confidence back. But her family wouldn't let her go; Sally Ann kept getting dragged back into the emotional black hole of her parents' constant crises until she was consumed by their overwhelming need and her own rigid sense of duty.

Her own hunger for success drove her to law school and then into her demanding career. She had fallen into the prevailing mindset of the educated classes, and believed that any woman who didn't have a paying job was little better than a parasite and leech. She drove herself to exhaustion, trying to be all things to all people—good employee, perfect wife, dutiful daughter.

Sally Ann thought, as she lay in the San Francisco hotel bed, that to some extent her father and then Luke had been catalysts for her new-found sense of well-being, if only because both had made things so bad for her that finally she had to change or be destroyed. Now that she didn't work for Luke anymore, her anger toward him was slowly fading although she knew she would never have any interest in seeing or speaking to him again.

She hoped one day to recapture her compassion for the sad and lonely man who had been her father. For now, though, most of her anger had been replaced by a feeling of cold emptiness on the infrequent occasions when she thought about him. She knew that she would have to heal herself before she could come to terms with her father.

Occasionally Sally Ann felt as if his spirit were visiting her, checking in to see how she was doing. She sensed his bewilderment as he tried to reach out to the daughter whose love he had rejected in life. Each time she felt his presence, Sally Ann asked him to go away. I'm not ready for this yet, she would mentally say. Maybe some day, but not now. We always did things on your terms while you were alive. Now we're following my agenda.

She had made the mistake of mentioning this to her sister Claire on one of the rare occasions when Claire telephoned. Her sister was, as always, judgmental and disapproving.

"I really think you're just wallowing in negativity," Claire said. "You should have some kindness toward Daddy's memory; you know what a sick man he was. You owe it to Dad to let him reach out to you, if that's what he wants."

Sally Ann had forced herself not to make a snide comment about the fact that Claire had sat out the family's bad years in Oregon, working to save the earth while Sally Ann coped with the daily reality of a severely depressed mother and senile, physically disabled father. "I gave Dad all my kindness when he was alive," she told her sister evenly. "Now I'm being compassionate toward myself."

Pressing herself more firmly against her sleeping husband, she sighed and thought drowsily before she finally fell asleep that Joe and Bubba were her real family. Their love for her, and her own strong sense of self, protected her from the cold void of loneliness into which so many people disappeared.

Dogs, Harleys and Facial Massagers

"So, what do you want to do today?" Joe asked the next morning. Since his wife and dog were with him, he had decided to stay in San Francisco over the weekend.

"We could take a stroll through the Castro and gross out all the gays by holding hands in public," Sally Ann suggested. "'Eeww, look, he's touching her,'" she said in an affected voice. "'Really, Chad, I just don't know where those people get off.'"

Joe laughed and pulled his wife toward him. "We could induce mass hysteria if I did this," he said, holding her with one hand and reaching under her T-shirt to fondle her firm bare breasts with the other.

"After all these years," Sally Ann said as she leaned into her husband's embrace, "you still make me get weak-kneed when you touch me."

"Good. I intend to keep on doing it." Joe kissed his wife deeply; Sally Ann felt his thick mustache pressing into her upper lip as their tongues probed each others' mouths. She pressed her hips into Joe's body, feeling his erection through his jeans.

Behind them Bubba whined and barked. "Oh, goddammit," Joe muttered as he reluctantly pulled away from Sally Ann. "Are you paying me back for getting you fixed when you developed doggie prostate trouble? Don't you remember the days when you used to chase poodles?"

Bubba barked again and looked expectantly toward the door, his tail wagging.

"Oh, all right," Joe said with amused resignation. "Wait a minute until I can walk and then I'll take you for a stroll."

"I'll finish getting dressed while you guys are out," Sally Ann said. "Then why don't we walk over to North Beach and look around."

Two hours later they were sitting in an outdoor café in San Francisco's renovated North Beach area, original home to the '50s Beats which had later deteriorated into a skin district before it was yuppified in the '80s. Sally Ann ate her salad with Gorgonzola and walnuts, while Joe enthusiastically plowed into his bacon-cheeseburger and fries.

"Well, hello," Sally Ann said as she heard toenails clicking on the terrace's Mexican tiles and a cold wet nose touched her ankle. She looked down into the eager little face of a brown ragmop on four legs. "I bet I know what you want."

"McGuane," a man's voice called from behind Sally's table. "Stop bothering the lady."

"He's not bothering us," Joe said. McGuane moved around to Joe who, asking 'do you mind?,' gave the dog a bite of sourdough bread.

Sally Ann turned around to see McGuane's owner, a well-built man with powerful shoulders and thick white hair pulled back into a ponytail. "McGuane," she said. "That's an interesting name."

The man's companion, a lithe, dark-haired young woman, laughed. "Oh, Bob's an old hippie from way back," she said. "He named our dog as an homage to one of his favorite authors from his glory days."

"He seems to be carrying the honor well," Sally Ann said, looking at the shaggy little dog who had made his way to the next table where he was begging for more handouts.

"Yeah, it hasn't gone to his head," Bob said as he stood up and put on a black leather jacket with silver rings attached to the front. "Come on, babe, we've got to get going or we'll be late."

"After all these years and all that dope you still haven't lost your middle-class obsession with timeliness," the woman said with fond amusement.

158 · N. E. JULIAN

"Yeah, well, only you young people can get by with being late all the time," Bob said ruefully as he laid enough money on the table to cover their bill and the tip.

The woman stood up gracefully, putting on her leather jacket as Bob called, "Here, McGuane!" The little dog obediently trotted over to them. Bob bent down and put a small black sweater with silver chains trailing from it onto his dog.

The three of them left the restaurant and got onto a large Harley parked by the curb. Bob and his lady friend put on the helmets they had left hanging on the motorcycle's handlebars, then seated themselves on the black leather seat with Bob in front. He reached over and picked up McGuane, placing the dog in front of him on the saddle, then clipped the silver chains trailing from McGuane's sweater onto the metal rings attached to his jacket.

Bob started the Harley, which fired up with a roar. He steered the motorcycle into the traffic, with the woman holding him around the waist and McGuane cradled tenderly against his chest.

Sally Ann and Joe watched until they could no longer see McGuane's brown ears flapping in the wind. "Looks like someone's got a rough life," Joe said.

"About as rough as Bubba's. We'd better not tell him about this, though, or he'll be jealous—he'll want his own Harley and a little biker sweater."

They finished their meal, then ordered coffee for Joe, tea for Sally. They sat in companionable silence enjoying the moment and the weak San Francisco sunshine that slanted across the restaurant's portico.

"Joe," Sally Ann said hesitantly.

"Yeah, babe?"

"I don't think I'm going to look for any more part-time law jobs. I can't go back to that life."

"I know."

"I really think that if I market myself, I can find several solo practitioners who'll send me their overflow work so that I'll still be bringing in some money."

"Well, you've made a start with Jon Rabinowitz."

"I'm sorry, Joe. I feel like I've let you down."

"You don't need to apologize, Sally. Over the past few months you've started turning into the woman I always knew was underneath your tough surface. Now you're starting to let other people see how happy and warm you can be.

"Besides," Joe added with a grin, "I know you don't have a neurotic need to be productive."

Sally Ann and Joe both laughed at his reference to a ghastly dinner they had endured the first night of their trip. They had gone to Green's at Fort Mason with a young partner from one of Joe's firm's new but growing clients. As they sat eating the restaurant's delicious vegetarian food and watching the evening lights play across San Francisco Bay, the client's wife had bragged endlessly about her small child and then patronized Sally Ann for having neither a baby nor a job.

The woman, who was a mid-level executive with an obscure insurance company, had clinched her comments by saying condescendingly to Sally Ann, "Oh, I do envy you your ability to stay home and do nothing. But I just have this neurotic need to be productive."

Sally Ann had looked with amusement at the woman as her husband turned red from embarrassment. "Yes, I can certainly see that you're full of neurotic needs," she had said with a quiet smile.

Joe signaled the waiter and asked for more coffee. Sally poured herself another cup of tea.

"I love you, Joe," she said. "I don't know if I could make it without you."

"I love you, Sally," he answered. "Don't sell yourself short. You'd get along fine without me . . . Besides, you'd never be alone. Some other guy would come along."

"I don't want another guy," Sally Ann said seriously. "I want you."

"I want you, babe," Joe answered. "And I need you. I'm glad we're together." He smiled lovingly at his wife. Sally Ann got tears in her eyes and her throat tightened. She started to make herself stop crying, then thought, What's wrong with a few tears? She reached across the table and took Joe's hands, smiling as two big drops slid down her cheeks.

"Besides," she said with a watery smile, "I couldn't go through housebreaking another husband. It took me years to train you and Bubba not to pee on everything in sight."

"On behalf of those of us carrying the Y chromosome, I resent that," Joe said, laughing.

"I've been scrubbing your bathroom for sixteen years," Sally Ann retorted. "I know what I'm talking about."

"What are you going to do with us males, Sally?" Joe asked teasingly. He pulled a piece of folded paper from his shirt's breast pocket and tossed it to her. "I found this ad in the coupons in this morning's newspaper. Would one of those substitute for a real guy?"

Sally Ann opened the piece of folded newsprint and saw a picture of a smiling young woman holding a vibrator pressed against her face. 'Suffering from tension?' the ad copy asked. 'Relieve stress with our patented facial massager—it comes in 7" standard and 10" deluxe models (batteries not included).'

"Yeah, right, facial massages," she said, then added, "God, ten inches—I bet I could really get a good massage with that. I have been feeling a little stressed lately." She looked at Joe and laughed. "Don't worry, sweetie, one of these wouldn't do me any good since it doesn't have a nice warm husband attached to it."

"Well, that's a relief." Joe smiled at his wife. "I'm glad I can't be replaced by a plastic tube and some batteries."

"Nope," Sally Ann said. "I couldn't talk to a 'facial massager' . . . or snuggle up next to one at night."

"You do build up my ego," Joe said.

"I try to be a good wife," Sally Ann replied. "But don't get conceited—Bubba's one hell of a snuggler." She smiled lovingly at her husband; Joe reached across the table and covered her small, loosely clasped fist with one of his big warm hands.

Behind them they heard a discreet cough. "Will you be needing anything else, sir?" their waiter asked.

"Just the check, please," Joe answered.

"What now?" Joe asked as he and Sally left the restaurant.

"Let's play tourist and walk around the city, then go back to the hotel and check on Bubba. After that, who knows?"

"Sounds good to me." Joe put his arm around Sally's shoulders, she put her arm around his waist, and together they set off to explore San Francisco.

Chapter Ten

Déjà Vu, But Not All Over Again

Halfway to Key West

Sally Ann left the Jenkins law library for a late lunch. She stepped from the building's lobby into the cheerful sunshine of an early summer day in Philadelphia.

As she strolled down the sidewalk on Chestnut Street, past the seedy stores and down-at-the-heels office buildings, she discreetly glanced from behind her sunglasses at any attractive man who crossed her path. Most of the male passersby, good-looking or not, were already staring at her.

For old times' sake, Sally decided to ride a bus to the former, and still missed, Twentieth Street Bar and Grill. She wondered if the disastrous Montego Bay was still usurping the site, or if the restaurant had been incarnated again into yet another pretentious theme eatery with bad food.

When Sally Ann left the bus, she looked down the street and saw what appeared to be a familiar striped awning sticking out over the sidewalk. She got closer, and saw 'Twentieth Street Bar and Grill—yes, we're back!' stenciled on the front window.

I don't believe this, she thought. This is too good to be true. Stepping through the main door into the almost-gloomy front seating area, Sally Ann stopped to let her eyes adjust to the light. She looked toward the end of the bar that divided the two dining rooms and saw a tall black man flirting with the male bartender.

"Aaron," she called. "Is that you?"

The man turned and smiled happily when he saw Sally. He grabbed a menu and hurried toward her. Sally Ann saw that Aaron was once again dressed in his urban waiter's outfit of black jeans and T-shirt.

"Well, well, well," he said when he reached Sally. "What's new in Ms. Straight White Chick's life?"

"What's new in yours?" she answered. "What happened to Montego Bay?"

"My God, what a disaster," Aaron replied with a shudder. "We lost all our patrons and most of the staff quit. The place almost shut down. Finally the owner sold the place to the former manager and he reopened the original restaurant."

"Well, thank goodness," Sally said. "I can't tell you how much I've missed coming here."

"You and a lot of other people. We're finally rebuilding our core of regular clients and the walk-ins are starting to come back for repeat visits."

Aaron took Sally Ann to her favorite table in the front corner of the restaurant, right by the picture window that overlooked the sidewalk and street. "Since it's summer, you want iced tea, I assume."

"How well you know me." Sally Ann smiled at Aaron. "Did you all go back to the old menu?"

"Pretty much. We have a new chef, but he's good. Do you want to hear the list of specials?"

After she gave Aaron her order, Sally Ann looked at the wall where the painted party scene had once hung. The painting was still gone, now replaced with travel posters from various Mediterranean countries.

"Where's the painting?" she asked Aaron when he brought her a basket of rolls.

"Everyone wants to know that. The old owner refused to sell it, mainly out of spite if you want my opinion. He was pissed because nobody appreciated his precious new restaurant. The last I heard, it's still hanging in his basement."

"What a waste. Oh, well, I guess we can't have everything."

"By the way," Aaron said, "I've been having a feeling I was going to see you. I cut this out from last week's newspaper. Have you already seen it?"

Sally Ann took the piece of newsprint from Aaron. 'PARROTHEAD ALERT!' huge headlines screamed. 'JIMMY BUFFETT COMING TO TOWN! FIRST LIVE CONCERT IN THREE YEARS!'

"Oh my God," Sally Ann said. "I missed this. He's really going to do a show here?"

Together they read the rest of the ad, which gave the concert date and the names of the ticket agencies.

"Look, babe," Aaron said, "tickets go on sale next Saturday."

"Well, I know what I'll be doing Saturday morning. Thank you, Aaron. If it weren't for you I wouldn't have known he's coming to town."

"Make sure you get an early start, Sally. Mike, the new bartender, is a Parrot Head. He said that when Buffett was here three years ago the 25,000 tickets to his concert sold out in 30 minutes the first day they went on sale."

Sally Ann glanced over at Mike. "He's cute, Aaron. Any possibilities there?"

Aaron looked coy. "Maybe."

"Well, good luck." Sally Ann picked up her iced tea glass. "Here's to love and lust."

"Amen to that. Let me go check on your order." Aaron, slightly flustered, bustled away toward the kitchen.

"This must be serious," Sally Ann thought. She glanced again at Mike, hoping that Aaron, who was a nice man, had found someone to share his life, or at least some of life's adventures. A patron sitting at the bar, seeing Sally Ann looking his way, smiled at her and raised his beer glass. Sally Ann smiled back but flashed her wedding rings at him. The man, who appeared to be a few years younger than Sally and whose face was quite easy on the eyes, turned away in disappointment.

Sally Ann looked out the window since Aaron still hadn't appeared with her food. She watched with admiration as a tall Philly cop strode down the sidewalk, noticing the set of his broad shoulders and how good his firm butt looked in his tight blue cop trousers.

She thought back to the day, over a year ago, when she had strolled behind another tall, muscular cop as a diversion on her way back to a job she hated. She realized how much her life had improved since then.

I think I'm halfway to Key West, she thought as she sat relaxing in the restaurant's unpretentious atmosphere. And I didn't even have to leave home to get here.

Sally Ann got up and walked over to the juke box. She put in her four quarters and selected her songs, ending with Jimmy Buffett's cover of James Taylor's 'Mexico.'

"My life is definitely looking up," she said.

THE END